DESTINATION BEDDING

ALLISON TEMPLE

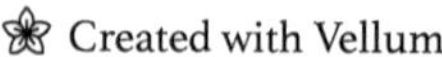 Created with Vellum

1

On principle, I, Katherine Marie Corriveau, am not opposed to dick. I've had my fair share in my life. Some big, some small. Wrinkly, smooth, pink, brown. Whatever. I don't judge based on looks.

Except it turns out I draw the line at green.

"Another round of cocktails, ladies?" The waiter puts the emphasis on *cock* while he smiles at our group with waggling eyebrows. Predictably, Claire and her friends all giggle. I roll my eyes and drop my gaze back to my half-finished rum and coke where the green penis straw stares back at me.

I check the time on my phone. Ten thirty-seven. Seven minutes since the last time I checked. How many more hours until last call?

When I glance up again, Claire is watching me, eyes narrowed, mouth pinched. She's been making that face her whole life whenever some part of her perfect plan doesn't live up to her expectations. Her friends bubble around her like a flock of improbable pink songbirds, decked out in their fake feathery boas and animal print dresses.

I give my baby sister my winningest smile as I slide my

phone back into my jeans pocket. No one told me I needed to dress for a theme. I run my hand over the worn denim, catching a fingernail on a loose thread where the knee has frayed. I'm in a small-town dive bar somewhere in the Colorado Rockies, surrounded by a menagerie of leopards, zebras, and tigers, and I look like I just rolled off the bus.

Which . . . technically, I have. Despite some not-so-subtle hints from Mom that arriving two days before Claire's wedding is the height of disrespect, I really didn't have another choice. Neither Claire nor Jono—excuse me, "Jonathan," since apparently he's an adult now—bothered to check with me when they set the date for their wedding. The festivities were very inconveniently scheduled for three days after my final exam. Getting out here to rural Colorado any earlier was impossible. And frankly, if it meant missing the final week of agonizing with Mom and Claire over the proper way to tie a chair sash while negotiating and renegotiating seating charts, I was more than happy to cruise into town at the last minute.

"Okay, girls." Madison, the maid of honor, stands on her chair. She's eschewed the general jungle mammal theme in favor of something that looks like a crocodile on acid. "It's time for a scavenger hunt!"

A fluttering of applause and excited whispers rustles over the table. We're about twelve people at this bachelorette monstrosity, including the bridal party and some of Claire's Denver friends who were able to come up early. Speaking of Claire, she's glaring again, which has me sitting up straighter and sucking harder on my penis straw to cover my mounting dread. Bachelorette parties really aren't my thing, but I've been to enough bars on a Saturday night to know the tasks on the pink sheets of paper Madison is holding will be stupid at best and humiliating at worst.

But once again, no one asked me.

And look, I don't *want* to be the sour sister at the end of the table, moodily sipping on a green penis while Claire's troop of friends gush about how excited she must be and how great she and Jono are going to look, and what time are we all getting together to have our nails done kin the morning and—

Since I tore two nails in my last practical exam while maneuvering a two-hundred-pound cadaver onto an embalming table, a manicure isn't going to save me.

Still, I didn't plan on playing the grinch, sucking all the fun out of the evening like a denim-clad black hole. I'd rather be making speeches about how my baby sister is all grown up and if her husband-to-be ever hurts her, I will hunt him down and break both his kneecaps before I ask questions, as any big sister would.

We'll just ignore the part where that very same baby sister is about to marry the guy *I* expected to marry not two years ago, and no one seems to think that particular plot twist is weird.

"So split into pairs," Madison is still speaking. "To get full points, one of you will complete the task, while the other takes a picture. Any questions?"

We all stand. I have the sudden rushing sense of déjà vu, like I'm ten years old and awkward all over again and my teacher has told us to pick a partner. I glance around for anyone I know won't be annoying to work with, while the clock in my head ticks down. One by one, Claire and the others assemble into pairs.

"So do we pick our own teams, then?" I ask.

Madison is standing next to Claire, their arms linked together. She smiles sweetly at me. "Didn't you get the email?"

I grimace. I was so caught up in studying that checking my email became an every-other-day-at-the-most kind of activity. When I logged in after my last exam, I'd been inundated by a hundred messages and replies, all with the subject line *Claire's Kick-Ass Bachellorete Party!!!!(Final Details!!!!!)!!!!!!!*

I was irritated by the spelling error and doubly irritated by the excessive exclamation points, so I skimmed the first message only long enough to confirm the date, time, and location, and then deleted the whole thread.

Except if I read everything, apparently I might have known about the scavenger hunt. And whose team I was drafted to. And that I was expected to come dressed like an ostrich, not a lumberjack.

"You're with me."

I freeze at the soft words behind me. I know that voice. Of the dozen or so of Claire's friends here tonight—along with the Denver contingent, the rest are mostly sorority sisters and a few girlfriends from high school—I only have any real connection with one, and that connection is more complicated than a tangled ball of yarn at a cat café.

I turn slowly, and Piper Petrescu smiles at me coyly from behind electric blue cat-eye glasses. Her dark brown hair is styled in soft curls that, along with her red lipstick, make her look like a pin-up model.

I've known Piper since we were kids, when she and Claire were in the same class. Sometimes, it felt like Piper lived at our house, but I never gave her much thought because she was just my little sister's friend. Another child to keep out of my preteen bedroom. A hanger-on during summer beach days, splashing and shrieking and drawing attention to our family when I was already too self-conscious by half.

These days, she's grown up into something completely different, and honestly, it's so much worse than the gangly little girl who snorted when she laughed.

"You're on my team." She pushes her glasses up, and I have to force back a shiver. Once upon a time, on a night not unlike this one, I spent an hour obsessing over that little gesture and wondering what it would be like to shake the bobby pins out of that perfect brown mane.

Then I'd gotten my answer and promised I'd never tell a soul.

I give Piper a tight smile. "Sounds like fun."

Madison beams and hands us a very pink checklist and a Sharpie adorned with feathers and glitter, most of which are promptly transferred onto my hand. Shit. I'm going to be smearing glitter for the rest of the weekend.

"Okay, everyone!" Madison puts her hands in the air. "You have one hour to complete everything. And don't forget, we all lose three points every time Claire doesn't have a drink in her hand."

More cheering. Piper and I stand next to each other with all the grace and enthusiasm of two ancient fence posts in a Scottish field. We must look like the ultimate odd couple. If I don't have to say it out loud, I can admit that Piper's grown into this curvaceous plus-size goddess and knows how to work every inch of her body, from the corseted top to her cherry red combat boots. I, on the other hand, am in head-to-toe black with no makeup and a haircut I maintain on my own with the number two setting on a pair of clippers I stole from my dad.

No one gives us a second glance, though, as they disperse into the crowd, ready to take this drunken merriment into its next phase. Hopefully, Madison has already assigned someone to the official role of Claire's hair holder while she pukes. My sister is petite in every way possible. Five-foot-two and maybe weighs a hundred pounds soaking wet. A couple more of those pink shots that keep getting passed around and she'll be placing a call to the porcelain gods in no time. Three years of med school, eighteen months of backpacking in parts unknown, and nine months of funerary sciences means I have dealt with my share of barf and bodily fluids. I don't need to take one for the team tonight. On reflex, I place a finger by my nose, realizing too late that now I almost certainly have glitter on my face.

Beside me, Piper giggles. I roll my eyes and thrust the marker and scavenger hunt list at her. I think I hear her say "Oh for fuck's sake," but I don't stick around to find out. Let her deal with the inadvertent glittering and all the humiliating things we're supposed to do to entertain my sister. I'm going to the bar.

Except as I order a fresh drink with no straw and turn around, Piper is at my elbow.

"What do you want?"

I probably shouldn't be such a bitch, but I'd been doing a pretty good job of ignoring Piper's presence, so getting saddled with her in the name of fun and games is not at all how I wanted to spend my night.

With a smirk, she slides up next to me. The bar is crowded. She says, "I wanted to talk to you."

I was hoping it was clear that is the exact opposite of what I wanted. If I'd wanted to talk, I'd have called her last year. Or followed her back on Instagram. In fact, the week after Claire's engagement party, I used my decade-old Facebook friendship with Piper—not that we ever did more than like the occasional picture or meme on each other's accounts—as the excuse I'd been needing to abandon my social media accounts entirely. Most were out-of-date anyway, and the rest had served their "fuck-you-Jono" purpose while I'd been abroad, at least until he one-upped me by marrying my sister. No need for them to reflect any of the bad decisions I'd made as a result of their engagement.

"What's on the list?" I ask. If I can distract her with one or two of these, we don't have to talk about other things.

Piper frowns, her lips sliding into a perfect Betty Boop pout. God, her lipstick. That night last year, it left perfect red rings around my nipples. Until Piper, I had never been a nipple kind of woman. Yet another thing Jono sucked at, apparently.

Piper, however, did not suck. Not at all.

I shake my head. Piper's said something, and I missed it because I was obsessing about her ruby red lips.

"I'm sorry," I say. "What was that?"

Her smile is amused, and I do not want to amuse her. I don't want to do anything with her. Ever again.

But she must feel differently, despite my months-long cold shoulder, because she says, "We have to kiss a guy. That's more your specialty than mine."

If you can get a repetitive strain injury from eye rolling, I'm probably very close to it. But fine. We'll play it her way if it means we don't have to talk. I tap the guy standing next to me on the shoulder, and when he turns around, I grab him by the shirt and plant a kiss on his lips. He looks stunned and pleasantly surprised as I let him go.

"What was that for?" he asks.

"Now what?" I say to Piper.

She pouts again. "We don't get full points unless there's a picture."

"Who cares about full points?" I want this over with as soon as possible.

Piper pushes her glasses up her nose, damn her. She says, "Well, if we're going to do this, I at least want to win."

I'm not sure why, but her words make my skin go hot.

"Are we really doing this?" she says breathlessly as I slam the door to the basement guest room shut behind us.

We did it. Been there, done that, don't have to do it again.

I grab the guy who is still waiting expectantly behind me, but this time I swing him around until he basically falls into Piper's arms. Nine months of lugging around dead bodies, along with eighteen months of "finding myself" with everything I owned in the world in an overstuffed backpack, means I'm stronger than most people expect.

I pull out my phone and point at Piper. "Your turn."

She looks like she's going to argue, especially when the guy holds out his arms and goes "Well, all right. Must be my lucky night."

"Ugh," Piper mutters. But almost before I can get the camera app open, she's reaching up for the guy's face and pulling him down to plant a bright red kiss on his open mouth. We've gathered a small audience—probably the people our willing victim is here with—and they cheer, which encourages him to ham it up a bit, giving me enough time to snap a picture.

Piper glares at me when she's done. I never asked her if she was into guys at all. Never asked her much of anything. By the time we started kissing, I was deep into my second bottle of Beaujolais. Chitchat didn't seem relevant.

She pulls out a tiny compact from the pocket in her flouncy leopard-print skirt and checks her lipstick. It is, surprisingly, perfectly intact. For good measure, and maybe because she knows what she does to me, Piper presses her glasses up her nose before she uses the glitter bomb pen to check off the first task on our list. Then she smiles at me sweetly and asks, "What do you want to do next?"

And because this wedding has completely fucked with my head, I ask, "Do you want to get out of here? Find somewhere quiet to be alone?"

Piper's eyes flash. Her corset squeezes her boobs up and makes them heave even more when she takes a deep breath. It looks uncomfortable, but the way they swell as she bites her bottom lip is something I have a hard time taking my eyes away from.

She asks, "What did you have in mind?"

I'm frustrated enough, or annoyed enough, or—okay, horny enough, it's been nothing but me and my fingers for months—that I say, "I think you know."

She arches a perfectly plucked eyebrow, and her curls bob as she leans into me. From a distance, she probably looks like she's trying to talk over the music, but I can't help the way I tremble when her lips brush my neck.

She says, "I thought I was a mistake."

And yeah, I did say something like that. I think I said "a lapse in judgment," which sounds slightly better than "mistake," but I'm desperate here in more ways than one.

I say, "I'm reconsidering."

She laughs in my ear, just once. Her hand creeps around my ribs and settles on my hip. Her thumb slides under the jersey of my T-shirt, brushing over my skin. My pulse starts to pound in my throat as she says, "I'll make you a deal. If we win this scavenger hunt, I'll take you back to my hotel room, and we can do anything you want."

What? No. Fuck. The whole point is not to do the scavenger hunt. Still, there was this thing she did with her tongue—

"Anything?" I say, sounding unbelievable needy. If the guy Piper just kissed was paying attention at all, he'd be ready to come in his pants as he watched the lesbian seduce the—whatever the hell I am—right in the middle of the bar.

It gets better when Piper gives me a catlike grin. She mouths the word *everything*, and I fumble with the front of my shirt because suddenly I don't know where to put my hands or look or anything. I'm such a mess. She makes me such a mess. From the moment Piper walked into Claire's engagement party and her gaze landed on me, I haven't been able to think clearly whenever she's close by.

"But why?" I say—okay, I whine. "We could go now."

Piper hands me the list and the sparkle bomb marker. "Because Claire is my friend and your sister, and we want her to have a good time, right?"

I eye her. Pout some more. My warming mood comes crashing down again, because right. We're here for Claire, and Piper was Claire's friend before I ever met her. Just like I was Jono's girlfriend when Claire wasn't even out of high school, and yet somehow, she still got the guy. This weekend is all about Claire and Jono and their perfect love and their bright future and—

I glance down at the checklist. Everything here makes my stomach turn. Get a piggyback from a boy. Find a boy who has the same name as the groom. Do a blow job shot between a boy's legs. I'm sorry, are there no adults at this party? Jono is a fucking pediatrician. Who uses the word *boy*? Why is this fun?

I turn to the guy next to me at the bar. He's different from Piper's kissing victim. Actually, he does look like a boy. I tap him on the shoulder, and his eyes go huge when he sees me.

"What's your name?" I ask.

"TJ." He twitches as he says it.

"Is it your birthday?"

He nods vigorously. "Yeah! I'm twenty-one today!"

I swing back to Piper. "Get your phone."

She frowns but does as she's told while I turn my attention back to the birthday boy.

"Want a ride?" I ask.

His eyes are so big they're going to fall out of his head. I'm a failed med student. I don't think I can treat that if it happens.

"Wh-what?" he stammers.

I turn and hunch, reaching awkwardly to pat my back. "Hope on. Birthday boys get a piggyback ride."

A few of his friends have noticed our conversation, and they're egging him on. One of them suggests maybe I can ride him instead—all night long. I think about a man I met while I was tending bar in Australia. He was Italian and very drunk and did not take no for an answer. I broke at least a couple of his fingers before it turned out he spoke English after all. I glance at TJ's friends. They're all about the same age, still growing into their limbs—and brains, unfortunately. But I can take them if I have to.

The boys—okay, yeah, they're definitely boys—cheer when TJ puts a tentative hand on my shoulder. I grin at him. "I'm stronger than I look."

His approach is awkward. I get a knee in the ribs. He's so tall that his toes almost touch the floor anyway, but I grunt as I face us toward Piper.

"Take the picture," I say, and she does, smiling bemusedly. TJ's friends whoop, and he stumbles as I straighten and set him back on the floor.

"I thought we were going for a ride?" TJ seems genuinely disappointed.

"Sorry, sweetheart." I pat his cheek. "Got things to do. Happy birthday."

His friends laugh at him, and I've probably spoiled his night. They're going to give him a hard time for hours. But I don't care. I check it off the list with flourish.

"What do you want to do next?" I ask.

Piper has her hands on her hips. "Technically, he was supposed to give you a piggyback ride."

No way. "That list is degrading to me as a woman. I'm not doing those things."

She taps her manicured nails on the boning of her

corset. "But if we don't do them, we don't win. And if we don't win, then you don't get to—"

"Yeah. Yeah." I wave her off. "We'll win. But I won't lower my standards for my sister's amusement."

A shout goes up across the bar. Near the dance floor, Madison is on her knees with her face in some guy's crotch. Claire is screaming unintelligibly as she holds her phone at an awkward angle, trying to capture the evidence. Madison throws her head back suddenly, and whipped cream leaks down the side of her mouth as she swallows her blow job shot.

I hate this so much. I hate it more when Claire's gaze meets mine and her smile grows wild. She screams again, throwing her hands up in the air like we're all having so much fun.

My sister and I have not had a single conversation, not a real one, since the night Jono told me he didn't think we were going to work out. And yes, I ignored her messages while I did the O circuit in Patagonia, and I didn't come home when she asked if I wanted to help organize Mom and Dad's thirtieth anniversary party. But even since I came back to the States last year, she's never asked me how I'm doing. Not once. And now I'm here, working up the nerve to shout "I need a guy named Jonathan!" at the top of my lungs so I can get something else crossed off my list for her entertainment, when she hasn't ever once asked me how I feel about any of this.

"Kate."

I jump at the sound of my name and remember that Piper is still standing beside me.

"What?"

"What's Claire's favorite song?"

"You're asking me? Surely this falls under friend trivia

you should know." I shrug. How would I know that? I don't know anything about my sister anymore.

Piper rolls her eyes and sighs before she tows me back to the bar. She orders four shots. One she hands to me, one she holds, and she nods at the bartender who takes a third.

"Bottoms up!" she says. I'm half a second behind her and the bartender. The whisky goes down fiery and vicious. It makes my eyes water, and I wheeze. Piper laughs and picks up the fourth shot glass before she grabs my hand again and pulls me through the crowded bar.

"She's still got a drink in her hand," I say as we go by Claire. In fact, she has two. Her veil is askew as she sucks on a purple penis straw.

"This isn't for her." Piper's curls bob as she leads us through the crowd of people dancing. I'm overheating in my shirt and jeans, but I can't take my eyes off the mole on her right shoulder. Every so often, her hair brushes against her skin just above it, and I wonder if it feels different. Of course, the medical training that once took up so much of my brain also wonders if she's had a dermatologist look at it, but that's beside the point.

To call the guy at the back of the dance floor a DJ would be generous. He's got a laptop open, but the way he keeps looking at his phone makes me think he's working from a "Friday Night Dance Party" playlist on Spotify. Yet when Piper hands him a shot, he takes it gladly, giving her a big smile, and downs it in one go. He leans in while she asks him something, trailing a hand over his chest. He nods, and they give each other a knowing fist bump.

"What was that about?" I ask when she comes back.

"You'll see." She winks and taps the side of her nose. She's definitely got glitter on her face, and I've reached halfway to her cheek to wipe it off before I even realize I've moved at all. She gives me another one of her knowing grins, and I finally have no option but to take off my flannel, tying it around my waist. Sweat drips down my spine, and when I brush a hand under my T-shirt, the skin is soaked.

As the song over the sound system comes to an end, a new one fades in. A scream goes up. Claire and three bridesmaids all rush to the dance floor, hands in the air and drinks sloshing as they start to dance wildly. People dancing around them have to give them a wide berth to avoid getting stepped on.

"Lucky guess. Okay, let's go." Piper pulls on my hand, and for a second I think she's finally caved and decided to take the opportunity to escape, but instead she takes me back to the bar.

"Go where?" I ask.

"That song is four minutes long. He's got one more cued up after that I know Claire can't resist. That means we have eight minutes to get as many of these things checked off our list as possible."

This is a diversion? "You're really serious about winning this?"

She kisses me. It happens so quickly that I have no time to prepare, and by the time I taste the edge of whisky from her lips on mine, she's already stepping back. I glance around to see if anyone noticed, but either they didn't or they don't care.

She says, "My hotel room is waiting." And part of me can't believe she still wants me. The moments we spent together last year are a heady rush of hormones and pure need, but the things I said after still make me flush with embarrassment.

Task #5: Get the DJ to play the bride's favorite song.

"Well played," I say, snapping a picture of everyone dancing. Piper doesn't hear my compliment though. She's already tapping a random guy on the shoulder and asking him if he'll buy her a drink. She does it with a bat of her eyelashes and squeezes her arms together to push her boobs up again. He's definitely not looking at her face as he waves down the bartender.

Task #6: Get a free drink.

She knows how to play the game, I'll give her that. Piper and her new friend do a cheers as I take their picture. He looks disappointed as we race off again, but I guess the beauty of this pseudo–destination wedding is we're never going to see any of these people again, so who cares if Piper breaks a few hearts along the way?

"We can do eight and nine together," I say, reading down the list. Eight is to write my phone number on the bathroom wall, and nine says to make a veil out of toilet paper.

Piper smiles as she finishes her free drink. "See? It's not so bad."

I scan the list for more items. "I'm still not doing the blow job thing," I say.

She wrinkles her nose. "Yeah, that one is pretty gross, I'll admit."

This time, I take her hand as we weave through the people. There's a line for the ladies' room, but we skip past it with repeated promises we don't actually have to pee. Fortunately, the first stall is out of order, so we help ourselves to the roll of toilet paper sitting on the back of the inoperable toilet. Piper takes one end of the roll and holds it to my forehead.

"Spin," she says, and I do, trying to maintain my detached disinterest, though a few giggles try to escape as the bathroom whirls around me. The paper breaks a couple times, but once we have a decent headband going, she goes about fashioning the veil part, leaving strips of white paper trailing over my shoulders and down my back in uneven lengths. When she's satisfied, she holds up her phone. "Say cheese."

I glance over my shoulder at her, glaring because no one can actually ever find out any part of this was fun. Piper, on the other hand, is positively beaming as she snaps the shot.

The music changes and my heart speeds up. Four minutes and our advantage is over.

"I need a pen!" I shout over the continuous murmur and laughter that is any women's bar bathroom on a busy night. No one seems to hear me or care. Piper reaches into the pocket of her skirt, and I expect her to hand me the glitter Sharpie, but instead she produces a tube of lipstick.

"Here," she says handing it to me.

It's red. Her red. When it emerges from the tube as I twist, it feels like an invitation.

I shake my head, trying to hand it back to her. "I'll ruin it."

"I have another one at the hotel. I never have only just one. It's my signature color."

And now I'm thinking about her lips again. She must know it, because the tip of her tongue drags over the lower one for a split second, and my whole body goes slack.

"Focus, Kate," she says, and I snap back to attention.

"This is so unhygienic," I say as I scrawl my phone number on the wall in bright red. "I really do need you to promise me you're never going to use this lipstick again."

She lines up the picture, with me standing next to my handiwork and pointing to it like a doofus in case anyone misses the scarlet smear. This time I do smile, only to remember too late I'm still wearing the damn toilet paper veil, which I swipe from my head as soon as she lowers the phone again. I scowl at her for not reminding me to take it off, but she laughs as she heads toward the bathroom door, leaving me with no choice but to follow.

"What else?" I ask as we re-enter the bar. We have to be nearly done, right? The song is reaching its height, and so are Claire and her friends. They're jumping up and down in a frenzy, though someone apparently is the designated drink refresher, because there's another pink shot in Claire's hand as she shakes her head and grinds on one of her friends' hips.

"Help me up," Piper says, holding out her hand, and I don't even have time to ask what for before she's hitching up her skirts, exposing the flouncy crinoline underneath, and stepping up onto a table near the dance floor.

"What are you doing?" I ask.

"Task number ten!" she shouts down. I glance down at the list.

Task #10: Dance on a table.

Piper's gaze is on the far side of the dance floor before she looks back down to me. "Hurry. Bouncer's coming."

"Okay, okay." I drop my phone as I try to get it out of my pocket. Every second I waste is a second away from getting Piper naked, and now I'm staring directly at her calves as she dances, and I'm imagining how soft her skin is and the way she'll laugh as I find the ticklish spot at the back of her knee and kiss it. When I first asked her if she wanted to get out of here, I was really hoping for some quick fun in a king-size bed and then we could both go on our merry way, but now I'm thinking, maybe we'll take our time and really get to know . . . well, not each other. We already know each other. This is a hookup, not anything more. But if she's willing, I'd really like to get to know myself and what I can do with someone like her.

"Help me down." She reaches for me, and when our eyes meet, I go so hot inside I think briefly about taking off my T-shirt too.

"Right. Yeah," I say, my brain whirring at a million miles an hour. "What's left?"

Task #11: Find someone with the groom's first name.

Damn. This one is going to be hard. Jonathan's not obscure, but it's not Dave or Steve.

Still, the music dies, and Claire and the bridesmaid squad start wandering off the dance floor. Our advantage is up. It's now or never.

"Jonathan!" I call into the crowd, looking for heads that turn faster than others. "Is there a Jonathan in the house? I need a Jonathan."

"Well, you don't have to ask twice," a voice says behind me. His voice is dark, warm, like good chocolate poured over cool ice cream.

Once again, I might hear Piper mutter "for fuck's sake," but I don't think about it very long as I slowly turn.

"Hey, Katie." He smiles. Once upon a time, that smile was all mine and made me feel like everything was right in the world. But even if it's directed at me now, it's not really mine to enjoy. It's Claire's.

Because standing behind me is Jono.

2

Jono. Jonathan Eric Holmes. I met him on the first day of undergrad, and by Christmas, I knew we were going to be together forever. When we got accepted to the same med school, that sealed the deal. We were going to save the world side by side.

"Jonathan!" The shriek is so ear-piercing, people around me flinch. Then Claire is hurtling toward us, a frothing purple snowball with murder in her eyes.

"Hey, Claire Bear," he says, laughing as she slaps at his chest.

"You're not supposed to be here," she says, stomping her foot impetuously. Or, it's probably supposed to be impetuous, except her balance is so bad it takes her three attempts before she manages to get that stompy little sucker back down on the ground. The cadre of friends have surrounded her and are all glaring daggers at him.

"I wanted to say hi," he says, smiling like this is the best joke he's heard all week.

"It's bad luck to see a bride at her bachelorette party," Claire slurs.

"Pretty sure that's not a thing," I say, but no one hears me.

"Aww, Bear Bear." He kisses the top of her head. I make quiet retching noises. Don't ask me what the hell is up with that Bear nickname; Jono said nicknames were juvenile when we were a couple.

Piper is watching me, and her lips are pressed into a thin, disapproving line. Figures. When Jonathan and Claire are together, they're like a giant black hole that sucks all rational thought away from anyone in their orbit. Suddenly, the only idea in anyone's head is what a perfect couple they are, no matter how disgustingly sweet and obnoxious they might really be.

Piper's disapproval means I'm not getting lucky tonight after all. Probably for the best. Things were less complicated when the only thing we had in common were childhood memories.

There's more squealing and laughing. Jono's best man, Tim, and another groomsman whose name I either never knew or have forgotten at some point show up not long after. They're supposed to be on some overnight camping adventure that is no doubt an excuse to drink in the bush. No one explains why they're back in town, but their arrival means the scavenger hunt is effectively over. Jono and Claire are glued to each other in the middle of the dance floor while their entourage circles them.

I sidle up to Piper, who's standing at the edge of their group.

"I'm calling it. We won," I say. "Time for my prize."

She glances down me, the lights reflecting wildly off her glasses.

"That's a terrible pickup line," she says.

Yeah, it is. I wasn't really expecting it to work. For a

minute, I'd actually been having fun there, but the moment is gone, and so is Piper's interest.

When the next song starts up, the whole bar erupts in a cheer, and even more people surge to the dance floor. That's my cue. I slip away and out the front door, leaving the blasting music and my sister's happy charade behind me. I'm still tired from the trip here, and at the back of my mind is a nagging reminder that the speech I'm supposed to deliver at Claire's wedding reception is unfinished.

Outside, the town sparkles. The mountains stretch over the tops of the buildings that line the street. For a minute, I think about going back to the hotel, packing up my stuff, and hiking up into the woods where it's quiet and the air is clear and I can think without the avalanche of emotions that always seems to hit me whenever I'm close to Claire and Jono.

But all I have back at the hotel is a wheelie suitcase with little more than enough clean underwear to get me through this weekend and the pink abomination otherwise known as a bridesmaid's dress hung up in the closet. Not even a backpack to stuff it all into. I won't get very far, and I'll probably get eaten by a wolf or a mountain lion for my trouble.

Instead, I let myself back into the hotel room. It's two double beds, and my aunt Lois is asleep in the one closest to the window. She's a motionless hump under the blanket and she's snoring gently, but when I turn on my phone's flashlight so I can find my way to my suitcase and get some PJs, she mutters in her sleep and rolls away. I take my stuff to the bathroom and get changed there with the door closed. Not that it takes much work. I sleep in an old T-shirt I bought at a gift shop in Malta. I wash my face, soaking the facecloth in water so hot it feels like my pores are weeping by the time I'm done, then stare at my reflection, trying to find the problem. The critical flaw that means I am incapable of having a good time this weekend. I got nothing.

Finally, I slip into bed.

Aunt Lois says, "You're supposed to be going doggy style in a bathroom with some hot young groomsman."

I freeze, clutching the blankets like a lifeline and stare up at the ceiling. If I don't say anything, maybe she'll believe I'm already asleep, even though I only just got into bed. Instead, she almost immediately starts snoring again.

Maybe Aunt Lois talks in her sleep? I wasn't supposed to crash with her, but when we got to the hotel, our room block was oversold, and it was either this or one of us was going to have to sleep in a yurt at the alpaca farm where we're having a picnic tomorrow. I actually volunteered for the yurt, but my mother deemed my generous offer to be disrespectful to my sister, and I got put in as Aunt Lois's roommate instead.

"The alpaca is eating my breakfast," Aunt Lois sighs.

Yup. Definitely talking in her sleep. I roll over, pulling the blankets up around my shoulders. It's spring in Colorado, and while the days are nice, the nights are cool, and Aunt Lois insists on sleeping with a window open.

My turn to sigh, though not about alpacas. That bachelorette party couldn't have gone any worse. I probably should have faked food poisoning and skipped it. Claire knows I'm no good at those kinds of things. Flirting with Piper was a recipe for disaster, especially since I was so awful to her last year.

Tomorrow. I will be better tomorrow. No more grumpy face. I will be the picture of sisterly joy and compassion. Paste on my best smile and wear it like the snuggest foundation garments for the next two days, and then I'm out of here and back to being my own person away from my family.

Tomorrow will be better.

IN FACT, tomorrow is not better. It starts at some ungodly hour with Aunt Lois tripping over her suitcase and swearing up a blue streak as she tries to get ready for the sunrise yoga class promised on the whiteboard in the hotel lobby.

"Come on, Kate," she says while I groan. "Since you're awake, you should join me. Stretch out those cobwebs."

"I'm only awake because you're talking," I say, burying my head under a pillow. I didn't even have that much to drink last night, but I still feel hungover. The idea of tipping myself upside down into a good downward dog sounds like a one-way ticket to vomit town.

"Oh, Katie," she says, jiggling my foot through the covers. "Don't be like that. You can't sulk around all weekend."

"Who said anything about sulking?"

"Katherine," she says. Or rather, she croaks. Aunt Lois is my mom's older sister, and while she swears she's never smoked a day in her life, she sounds like she's been nursing a pack a day habit since before she hit puberty. "I've known you since you looked like a squishy pink alien in your mother's arms. I know what it looks like when you're sulking."

I roll the pillow off my head. Lois is standing at the foot of the bed. She's in a gray crop top and a pair of flared spandex pants with a kind of beaded skirt sewn around the waist. Her gunmetal hair is pulled back with a bright pink scarf, but it's doing a very good job of trying to escape. Her skin is tanned and freckled from a lifetime spent outside, working in other people's gardens. Aunt Lois is who I aspire to be when I grow up—though I'm already twenty-nine, so by many people's measures, I'm already there. I shudder at the thought. I should get special dispensation since so many of my years were dedicated to a path that got thoroughly derailed through no fault of my own. I demand a makeup test.

For now, though, I crawl out of bed. I promised to be good today, and based on the way she was heading last night, there's very little chance of us running into Claire this early. The bridal party is booked in for a manicure midmorning, and that is likely the first time I'll have to face my baby sister today.

"Give me five minutes," I say.

We go downstairs together. The hotel is what you would expect for the primary accommodation at a ski resort. Lots of high ceilings and exposed beams. Paintings of mountains, forests, and the occasional salmon, with bronze sculptures on pillars depicting brave cowboys doing intrepid things back in the good old days.

At the bottom of the stairs, we're greeted by my mom, who is pacing across the hardwood lobby floor.

"Katie, Lois, good, you're up. There's a serious problem."

Beside me, Lois groans softly, which leaves me hiding a smile. A lot of what my mom perceives as serious problems would be viewed by the world at large as minor inconveniences. She once made me drive three hours home the weekend before midterms because she couldn't decide what color of yellow to paint my bedroom. The bedroom that she had designated as her new craft room. I tried to point out that since it wasn't my room anymore, I really didn't need to have any input on the paint color. Mom was deeply offended.

"Katie. I'm trying to honor your legacy. How am I supposed to guess if you'd be more comfortable with American Cheese or Amarillo?"

My legacy. Like I had died or cured cancer. Or both. Also, she had to repeat the question a few times before I realized she was talking about the names of paint. In the end, I'd picked American Cheese because I knew it made her uncomfortable to have to tell her friends that was the color on her new craft room walls.

"What's going on?" Aunt Lois asks, also accustomed to managing Mom's crises.

"It's Lynette," she says. This is Mom's younger sister. Lois, Leanne, and Lynette. They couldn't be more different. Lois is a landscaper on Long Island. She's unmarried, and while she's brought a plus-one to the occasional function, I've never met any of them more than once. Lynette is the baby. She's twice-divorced, and two years ago she moved to Switzerland to marry a banker twenty years older than she is. And Mom is Mom. She got married at the right age and had two girls pretty much straight away. She ran a daycare out of our house until she herniated a disk a couple years ago after too many trips up and down the stairs carrying a toddler who didn't want to walk anymore.

"What's wrong with Aunt Lynette?" I ask, because—yes—I'm trying to be good today.

"It's the surrogate," Mom says. That's all she says. She's got her arms out wide and her hands splayed like she's waiting for our reaction of shock and disappointment.

"What about her?" Lois asks. Lynette and her husband wanted a baby, but Lynette's in her late forties, so carrying one herself wasn't an option. They've hired a surrogate who's doing it, which, honestly, I think is pretty cool.

"She's in labor," Mom says, screwing her face up like she's eaten a lemon. "Lynette called. She got as far as London and canceled her flight. She's on her way back to Bern right now."

"That's amazing!" I say, because it feels like the thing someone should say. Honestly, I haven't seen Lynette since . . . gosh, I'm not even sure. Definitely not since I got back from my trip. I didn't even see her while I was in Europe. So maybe not since . . .

Ugh. My stomach goes acid. Not since my engagement party to Jono the summer before we started med school.

"It's not amazing," Mom says. "It's a disaster. Who's going to sit next to Grandma at the reception?"

Lois and I throw each other a knowing look. Maybe we do some mental Rock Paper Scissors. It's a valid debate. She's the eldest sister. I'm the eldest daughter. One of us has to talk Mom down.

Finally, Lois puts her arm around Mom's shoulders.

"Come on, Lee," she says. "Let's go get some coffees, and we can go over the seating charts again." The look she throws me over her shoulder as they walk away is very clearly *You owe me*, and I truly do.

And suddenly, I'm by myself in the hotel lobby. The obvious choice is to go back upstairs and catch a few more hours of sleep. Maybe work on the speech I still haven't started. One of the many bridesmaidly duties I've been avoiding. But I'm up and dressed, and the sun creeping through the windows does make the idea of sunrise yoga pretty appealing. The whiteboard says it's outside in the Granite Courtyard, and a helpful woman at the front desk points me in the right direction.

Outside, the air is crisp, but another woman with a high ponytail and cropped pants is setting out equipment, including cozy-looking woven blankets. A couple other people are milling around or seated on mats stretching. It all looks really nice and peaceful when I've felt anything but peaceful since arriving here.

"Good morning," a voice says behind me, and I jump.

Of course, it's Piper. She's in soft sweatpants and a T-shirt that's been tied off around her rib cage. Her hair is pulled up in a polka-dotted scarf, and this morning, she's wearing a pair of chunky square rainbow glasses.

"Hi," I say, not really sure where to look, because even with no makeup on, her face is amazing, and the swatch of bare skin between the knot in her shirt and the strip of her waist band is so inviting, and also—yeah—I may be a little embarrassed about last night. "I didn't expect to see you this morning."

Honestly, I was hoping to see her as little as possible. I can't seem to always put coherent sentences together when she's around.

She shrugs like I didn't say something rude. Piper's got a teal yoga mat tucked under one arm and she rolls it out at the back of the group.

"I left not long after you did," she says. "It's going to be a big day today."

"What about Claire?" I ask, looking around, in part because what if my sister is lurking in the bushes, and in part because I can't decide if it's rude of me to go find a mat somewhere else in the group or if I'm now committed to sticking by Piper's side—again—for the entire class.

"She and Jonathan were having a good time." The glance she gives me almost looks apologetic, and it leaves me annoyed. I don't want pity.

"What about it being bad luck?" I ask.

She smothers a laugh, which makes me feel a little brighter. Maybe we don't have to be awkward with each other all weekend. We are—as Piper continues to prove—adults. No reason to be immature. We don't need to do more than make small talk and pretend the matching pink lace and chiffon dresses hanging in our closets really are—as Claire continues to insist—something we'll wear again in the future.

At the front of the group, the instructor claps her hands, calling us together. I guess I'll be practicing next to Piper after all. But it's not so bad. We start with a gentle sitting meditation. I spent three weeks in Portugal last year right before I came back to North America, and I made a point of meditating every day. It helped manage the anxiety of the final few weeks before I flew home, but I haven't been as good about doing it since I started school again. Then the instructor takes us through some gentle poses that slowly work the knots out of my shoulders and add length to my spine. I focus on taking long deep breaths, feeling my feet press down onto the mat while I reach my arms over my head.

"Now put your hands on the ground and push back into downward dog," the instructor says, and I do, looking at my toes. They're calloused, and the nails are chipped. The spa will have their work cut out for them. I lost the nail on my baby toe somewhere in South America, and it's never grown back straight. Sort of like me after Jono broke my heart. The thought makes me laugh softly to myself. My whole life, I thought I was only attracted to . . . well, boys my age, and later to men. And then Jono ripped up the whole gameplan, leaving me questioning everything. Literally. Everything. And those questions had culminated with me and Piper necking in the basement while people toasted Jono and Claire's happy future one floor above us.

The instructor tells us to lift one leg and tip it over our hips, which makes me twist to my right. Piper faces away from me. Her foot dips down gracefully, and her ponytail drags on the ground. For a second, I have a memory of her hair dragging over my shoulders in a dark room, and I shiver. Her T-shirt has slid farther down her back, leaving her skin exposed. She's got a tattoo that looks like a swan in flight over the middle of her torso. Its neck stretches elegantly upward, back underneath the shirt. I don't remember that being there, but maybe it was because I was too rushed, too out of my mind with . . . everything . . . to notice.

I'm noticing now, though. We drop our feet and lift the other, turning in the opposite direction. I can hear her long exhalation and I try to do the same, but my heart has started beating faster. Is she looking at me? I force my leg around a little farther. I've got good legs. All that walking. Good shoulders from school. Does she like what she sees?

"Okay," the instructor says. "Now come back up to standing and find a partner."

A what? Why is everyone so obsessed with pairing up this weekend? It's like they're pumping heteronormative monogamy into the air to make sure Claire and Jono's special day is everything they could hope for.

My toe snags on the mat as I bring my foot forward and I nearly wipe out entirely, landing on my chin. But I manage to get myself upright, though the tension is back in my shoulders. Piper's standing with her hands on her hips. Her face is flushed, and while I spin around trying to find anyone else to partner with, she waits patiently for me to realize once again that the others are already paired up.

"Hey, buddy," she says with an immaculate arch of her eyebrow. "You ready?"

For her? For her soft stomach and her strong hands? For the way she wets her lips like she knows I'm one emotional crisis away from collapsing into child's pose and crawling across the ground to kiss her toes?

"Ready as I'll ever be."

3

"Have you ever done this before?" I ask.

She grins as she slides the bra strap off my shoulder. Her lips on my skin are hot, and I shudder at the contact. Everything about tonight is too much. Too loud, too warm. But as Piper's hands wrap around me to unhook the clasps along my spine, I think maybe this moment will be just right.

"Have you ever done this before?" I ask, eyeing her.

The sparkle in her eyes says she remembers me asking the same question before.

"I don't think it will be too intense. Not unless you want it to be."

I have to look away and pretend I don't hear the invitation. Because it had gotten too intense last year. One second, the only thing I wanted in the world was for Piper to never stop touching me, and the next, the panic had set in, and I couldn't get far enough away from her. Not her fault. Totally mine. But this is just yoga. We don't have to rehash what happened behind closed doors in a moment of weakness.

It's not too bad at first. We start seated, the soles of our feet together while we grasp each other's wrists. It's nice. I pull gently, and Piper pulls right back. The instructor offers guidance to others, and I let my eyes wander, watching people young and old as they find the stretch. The sun is over the mountains now, making the edges of the skyline feel sharp.

"Now take a deep breath and pull your partner to help them fold forward," the instructor says. Piper and I glance at each other, and I slowly pull until she bends at her hips. She lets me pull her until her nose is on the mat between us.

"Dear god," I say.

She laughs and her cheeks are flushed as she sits back up again, and we reverse the position. I don't fold as far as she does.

"Breathe," she says. I try to, but as I drop another inch or two, I find myself face to face with the inside of her thighs, and it really is very difficult to breathe like this. She kissed my thighs once, and now I'm wondering if I returned the favor. Her skin would be so soft. It has to be. She'd smell sweet, and she'd gently—

"And sit up again," the instructor says, and as I straighten, I truly am breathless. Piper's watching me like she knows exactly what I've been thinking. She lets go long enough to straighten her glasses, and I glance around. No one here is from the wedding.

The instructor tells us the next pose is called Temple. It involves standing facing each other, then bracing our forearms together and pointing our hands upward while we bend at the waist. The end result is that Piper and are inches apart. Her ponytail falls over her shoulder, dangling between us. Her gaze is on a point below my chin. The collar of my shirt is tight enough she can't see down the front of it, but when our eyes meet, her cheeks are once again bright pink.

"We should talk," she says finally, which isn't really what

I wanted her to say. Not right now, when we're so close and her lips are shiny and parted as she breathes carefully.

But she's right. I can lust after her all I want, but I'm here for Claire and my family. Now is not the time to be a bad bridal party cliche. And it's definitely not the time to revisit my sexual identity crisis.

Because here's the thing. That time with Piper? It's been the only time. I was drunk and angry, and she was the only one who seemed to pick up on it. God knows I had lots of offers in various bars and hostels around the world. I even kissed a woman in Oslo at New Year's, but it didn't go any farther than that.

There's something about Piper that makes my brain melt. But it wasn't always like that. When she and Claire were little, I certainly never noticed her as anything other than the awkwardly tall friend in Claire's preteen posse. She had a fondness for pigtails and wore braces longer than most of the other girls. But this grown-up Piper, the one I first saw at Claire and Jono's engagement party, with her curves and confidence and a come-hither look that makes me go weak . . . She's a different animal entirely.

I'm letting myself get carried away, though. All she's said is that we should talk.

I finish yoga, lying on my mat, letting myself relive the feeling of her breath on mine, her hands on my thighs and her tongue on my body as she—

"Did you fall asleep?"

I open my eyes and the yoga instructor is standing over me, smiling. I wrinkle my nose and fake a yawn to hide my discomfort.

"Must have," I say. "You should take it as a compliment."

She grins and walks away. Beside me, Piper has already rolled up her mat and is passing it to the instructor who thanks her. Then Piper holds a hand out to me, and maybe we're only going for coffee, but the gesture feels like an invitation.

"Come on," she says. "Let's get out of here."

———

THERE'S a coffee shop on the main drag in town. Piper gets a latte and a croissant breakfast sandwich with prosciutto and cheese. I take an americano and dump about eight packs of sugar in it.

"You're not hungry?" she asks as we sit down in over-stuffed couches.

I shrug. "I'm not much for breakfast."

She grins. "I disagree."

"Excuse me?" Pretty sure that's not a point up for debate. I eat what I want, when I want.

"I remember you crashing Claire's tenth birthday at the pancake house."

"Uh, I wasn't exactly crashing. I was fourteen and my parents were still legally required to look after my well-being, including making sure I received proper nutrition. What was I going to do? Make my own toast at home while you guys got high on silver dollars and whipped cream?"

She smiles as she takes a sip of her coffee. This all feels almost normal. Girlfriends having a coffee and shooting the shit. I don't really have girlfriends. Not anymore. I have online friends who text occasionally, but being off the continent for nearly two years, coupled with the fact most of my anecdotes these days involve corpses, and it really feels like the people I was closest to are off living different lives.

"So," Piper says as she bites into her croissant.

"So," I say.

"Are you still in love with him?"

I snort on my americano. "What?"

"Hey, guys! Good morning!"

I'm still mopping coffee off my face, but Piper is already looking toward the coffee shop door where Jono and Claire have just walked in.

"Oh, for fuck's sake," I mutter, and Piper gives me a wry look.

"Him," she says. "Are you in love with—"

"Yeah, yeah. Keep your voice down." I hunch into my hoodie as they walk toward us. Piper waves and smiles like it was her plan for us to meet here all along.

What if it was?

I eye her, looking for signs of her betrayal, but her glance in my direction is equal parts pleading and guilt, like she's afraid I'm about to make a scene, but also sorry she can't protect me better. Not that it's her job. It's mine. I'm the one looking after me. In fact, I'm very good at it.

Behave. Behave. I said I'd behave today.

"Good morning." My face hurts as I force a smile. "Didn't think we'd see you so early."

Claire laughs a pixie-dust smile. "Jonathan said we needed to go running."

"It's good for the nerves. We're t-minus thirty hours until ceremony time. Gotta stay focused." He takes a deep breath and slings an arm around Claire and they laugh, though I'm not sure what's so funny about running. Jono was always athletic. Even when we were pulling all-nighters studying, he'd always go out for a run at sunrise. Actually, I should have known we might bump into them, since sunrise runs and sunrise yoga typically happen at the same time.

"And we promised Madison we'd bring her a macchiato," Claire says. "She's a little . . ." She puffs out her cheeks and makes gagging sounds. Apparently, not everyone escaped the wrath of the pink shots last night.

"You feeling okay today, Katie?" Jono asks.

"I'm fine," I say too quickly, then punctuate it with more coffee. Between what I spat out and what I've swallowed, I'm already halfway through. If they stand here much longer, I'm going to regret not having a snack to keep my hands and my mouth busy. When I glance up again, he's still looking down at me—and Piper's watching me too. The only one who doesn't seem interested in my well-being is Claire, who has already wandered over to the counter to place an order.

"My parents are arriving this morning," Jono says. "Mom's looking forward to seeing you."

If my coffee cup were paper instead of ceramic, I'd crush it. But I say, "It will be nice to see her again too."

Of all the things I lost when our engagement ended, Jono's mom might be the one I missed the most. My mom's always been closer to Claire than to me. Not that she was a bad mom or anything, we just don't have much to talk about, especially not now. Jono's mom always seemed to get me.

"Jonathan!" Claire calls. "Do you want a carrot or a banana muffin?"

He smiles down at me, then seems to remember Piper is here too, and gives her a grin. "I'll see you both later at the picnic."

When he's gone, we don't say much. Piper finishes her sandwich. I nurse the bottom third of my coffee.

Finally, Piper says, "If you're still in love with him, you should say something before tomorrow."

I roll my eyes. "Firstly, this isn't a movie where he's going to admit it's always been me and we run away together. Especially not when he had me and gave me up. And secondly, I'm not in love with him. I have better self-esteem than that."

She considers this as she picks at crumbs on her plate. "But you're mad at Claire."

I nearly ask who wouldn't be but manage to hold that back. Because that's not exactly it either. It's not like she stole my man. But also, she didn't ask me. No one's asked me. No one's said anything. On a random Saturday in July last year, I got off a plane and showed up at Mom and Dad's, only to be informed I was just in time for Claire and Jono's engagement party that night. No one had invited me. They hadn't even mentioned it when I'd called to say I was buying a ticket back to the States.

No wonder I'd been out of it enough that when Piper had offered more than small talk and platitudes, I'd taken her up on it.

Which does beg a question now.

"What does it matter to you?"

She shrugs, like she was expecting me to ask. "Claire's my friend. I want her to have a good time at her wedding. But I've known you just as long. It looks like you could use a friend too."

Her sincerity makes me itch. I don't know anyone else in this coffee shop, but somehow, I feel like every eye is on me. The whole place is collectively holding its breath.

Well, I'll give them something to talk about.

I reach across the table, wrapping my fingers around Piper's. Her eyes widen and her nostrils flare.

"I'm sorry for what I said that night."

She squeezes my hand . . . or maybe it's more like a flinch. That wasn't my finest moment. The making out was great. Piper found me hiding in the guest room—what with my room being overrun with scrapbooking and quilting supplies—and she offered me a lifeline. Or a distraction, I don't know. The first time she kissed me was like an out-of-body experience, and I'd given up control. It felt good, touching her, letting her touch me. For a while, I didn't have to think about everyone upstairs. People I'd known my whole life. People who either talked to me like they still knew who I was, or else they couldn't quite make eye contact while they asked me how my vacation had been. A vacation. Like I'd packed off to the beach for a weekend.

Of course, then, as the glow had worn off and I realized I was lying in bed with a girl I'd known since she was probably eight years old—never mind she was most definitely all grown-up now—a cold wash of panic poured over me. Because they were all upstairs and someone was bound to notice I'd disappeared. And Piper had rolled over and smiled at me with sleepy bedroom eyes and said, "I've been wanting to kiss you since the first time I realized I was queer," and . . . yeah. Panic. While I struggled back into my clothes, I told her I'd made a lapse in judgment. Then cold-shouldered her for the rest of the night—in my defense, I cold-shouldered everyone for the rest of the night—and haven't spoken to her since. Not until she appeared at the party yesterday.

She stacks her cup on top of her plate, then takes my mug too. I wonder if she's ever worked in a restaurant and does it to save the servers a step or if she's been taught to be polite.

But her voice is matter-of-fact when she says, "I'll make you a deal. If you want."

"If I behave myself around Claire and Jonathan, you won't tell my nearest and dearest I'm bisexual?"

Her brows crease, and I immediately regret the words. She wouldn't do that.

"Sorry," I say. Without the mug to drink from, I start peeling a paper napkin into strips. "I . . . no one knows about that." No one here this weekend, anyway. No one on this continent. Talking with my family about anything since I came back has been awkward, and now is not the weekend to come out of the closet. Ick. The very phrase makes me feel ashamed. I'm a strong independent woman who should own her identity. But if I decide that this is the weekend to tell my parents I'm bi, my mom will accuse me of trying to steal the spotlight from my sister on her big day. And maybe she's right.

Piper clears her throat. She says, "I'll make you a deal." And this time, I keep my thoughtlessness to myself. "For every family event you have to go through this weekend, we can do anything you want after."

My throat goes dry. I'm filled with memories of her next to me, wrapped around me, holding me. She smelled like cinnamon and red wine. Though the red wine might have been me.

"Anything?" I ask.

She bites her bottom lip. "Mm-hmm."

"What if I want to . . . hike up into the woods and sleep under the stars?"

The corner of her mouth quirks up. "We might need to bring some bear spray or something, but we can do that."

"If I want to go midnight skinny dipping in the river?"

She shivers but nods.

I glance around. We're still functionally alone. No one notices as I wrap my other hand around hers and press my lips to her knuckles.

"And if I wanted to—"

"Yes." She nods vigorously. "Definitely that."

"Even though I was awful to you last time?"

"I knew that wasn't really you. It was a weird night." She unravels our hands and picks up the dishes, carrying them back to the counter. I trail after her, feeling a bit like a kid given a gift I'm not allowed to play with yet. But for the first time since my plane touched down in Denver, I feel like maybe this weekend won't be so bad after all.

"So do we start now?" I ask, as we walk down the street.

"Since we just ran into Claire and Jonathan? I feel like I deserve something for not calling him a spineless weasel to his face."

"You're sure you're not still in love with him?"

The question stops me in my tracks. I gape and gawk and finally cross my heart and mimic zipping my lips shut. She rolls her eyes, but before I can plead my case, she grabs me and tugs me into an alley separating the coffee shop from the next building and pins me up against the wall. Her mouth on mine tastes like salt and butter, and it's heavenly.

And too short.

Before I can really begin to enjoy myself, Piper pulls away. I pout and she grins.

"That was a freebie." She points a warning finger at me. "Chance encounters aren't part of the deal, or else we'll never get anywhere."

"Now you're talking," I say, swaggering toward her, but she laughs as she pushes me back a step.

"Planned events only. No more rewards for running into people in the hall or at the pool or in the street. Got it?"

I huff, but it's not like I'm going to say no. Not when I can still taste her against my lips. Not when I'm reminded of how good it feels to have her and all her soft curves pressed up against me.

"Got it."

"Good. Now let's go. Manicures in fifteen minutes."

4

I was right. The woman doing my pedicure takes one look at my feet and calls in the big guns. Claire, Piper, Madison and the two other bridesmaids all need cute little files and delicate clippers. I need something that looks like a power tool to grind off the callouses, and I'm pretty sure the clippers she pulls out could be used to crack open my sternum in an emergency.

"All that hiking," I tell her apologetically as she hacks at my feet.

"I thought you worked at a funeral home?" Madison asks, before Claire nudges her.

I smile blandly. "I'm still studying funerary sciences. Someday I'll work at a funeral home."

One of the other bridesmaids squeals. It's a common enough response when I tell people what I do now. Even the woman grinding my feet glances up at me uncomfortably. Honestly, I'd rather deal with a dead body than I would a living person's gnarly feet any day of the week.

The bridesmaid says, "I thought Claire said you were a doctor. Like Jonathan."

"Melissa!" Claire sounds exasperated. "That's not what I said."

She probably said I dropped out of med school because Jono broke my heart. Or maybe that I broke his. Makes it seem more plausible that she would be there to pick up the pieces that way. I stuff the thought back down. I'm not always like this. Most of the time, when I'm sitting through an embalming lecture or wandering the trails in the Hudson Valley, I don't think about Claire and Jono and their happy future. It's only this weekend, when they're in my face all the time and that very same happy future is about to collide with the present, that I'm at my bitchy best.

Speaking of which, my efforts to blend in are still failing. Piper and I made it back to the hotel in time for me to run upstairs and change before we had to walk down to the spa. Because the event after this is a picnic, I've gone with jeans, a T-shirt, and a lightweight down jacket. All black, of course. Piper showed up in denim pedal pushers, a plaid shirt once again tied up to expose a strip of skin above her waistband, and a green cardigan. I suppose she represents some kind of middle ground between me and Claire's athleisure posse. Still, if one of these things is not like the other, that thing is definitely me. Piper's clothes, while not some techno moisture-wicking fabric, are still chosen and cut to accentuate her shape. Mine only do that if we acknowledge I am the approximate shape of a potato.

Though I really am digging Piper's style. I make a mental note to ask her the next time we're alone when she started dressing like this. It's got a cute vintage vibe that works for her, and when I glance to her in the chair next to mine, one of the buttons of her shirt is struggling to stay in line with its colleagues, leaving a gap just wide enough for me to catch a glimpse of the bright red bra beneath.

Anything I want. That's what she said.

I'm last to finish up with the pedicure, and they move me over to a small table for the manicure. I'm seated next to Claire, who is chatting a mile a minute with her manicurist.

"I was ready to go home, but he was so insistent that he had to keep going. I had blisters for a week after because of the rain. But then we got to the top of the mountain, and he got down on one knee and proposed." She sighs. "It was perfect."

"Sounds like it," the manicurist says as she paints Claire's nails with clear polish. "How did you two meet?"

Even strangers must be able to feel the awkward silence that follows. Claire stares straight ahead as the tiny brush glides over her nails. Madison and Melissa are whispering to each other. But Piper actually looks like she might not have heard, and the bridesmaid next to her is still talking to the woman across from her too, so maybe I'm overreacting.

Still, Claire has to clear her throat and paste on a smile before she says, "I met Jonathan when I was in high school. We've known each other for a long time."

Uh-huh. All true and yet so very false. Also, what's with the mountain climbing story? Claire doesn't even like to hike. And showy proposals aren't Jonathan's style either, at least not with me. When he proposed to me, it was literally as we were walking into our last final of undergrad. He said, "When this is all over, let's get married," and then I nearly bombed the exam because I couldn't stop thinking about whether he meant when the test was over, like we were going to run off in the middle of the afternoon and elope, or if he meant after we were done with med school, or after the fall of humanity.

"How do you know the bride?" my manicurist asks.

I give her a tight smile. "I'm her older sister."

"Oh, that's so fun. Are you married too?"

Okay, this time the silence is such that even the woman

scrolling on her phone by the reception desk looks up. Claire's gaze is still on her hand, while the others are all watching me like I've just been asked if I know who had the last slice of cake while there's chocolate frosting smeared all over my mouth.

Mustn't do anything to upset Claire's big day.

"No. I haven't found the right person yet."

So yeah. That's pretty much how the rest of our pampering goes. The bridesmaids pick up the chatter, and I say nothing, and it looks like we're all going to get out of this unscathed when Claire's phone starts to ring. A quick glance says it's Jono's number, and I can't handle sitting here listening to them have some sticky sweet conversation, so of course Claire—who has one hand in the dryer and the other being painted—asks, "Katie, can you get that?"

No. Please no. Anyone else. And how is it that I sat down to have my nails painted last, but somehow, I'm already done and Claire's still a work in progress?

But the phone's still ringing and there's no one else closer, so I sigh and pick it up.

"Hello?"

"Hey, Bear Bear. You ready for me?" He makes a growling sound, and I have to close my eyes to keep breathing.

"It's . . . it's not Claire. It's Kate."

"Oh. Shit. Kate, hi." At least he has the decency to be flustered.

"Claire's still having her nails done. Can I help you with anything?" This may be the longest string of words I've said to him since the night we broke up.

"Uh. Yeah. Sorry. Uh." He's talking in a circle, which is as off-putting as it is annoying. Jono is always supremely confident. You don't get into med school and get a placement at your top choice hospital by being a pushover. To hear him scrambling for something as simple as a phone mix-up makes me question for the hundredth time this weekend if I actually know him at all. "Shit. Sorry. Claire said I was supposed to call and make sure you were done and on your way to the picnic."

I glance down the row of tables. The others are finished.

"We're just waiting on Claire," I say.

"Great. That's great." He sounds relieved. "I'll, uh . . . I'll see you at the farm, then?"

When he says *you*, I have to tell myself he doesn't mean me specifically. The plural *you*. All of us. We're essentially a six-headed bridal party monster. Interchangeable, except for Claire.

"Yeah," I say, as Claire makes hissing noises.

"I need to talk to him." She reaches for the phone, but as she does, her hand brushes the edge of the lamp that's hanging over the workstation, leaving a gouge in her polish. She makes a dismayed noise, and the manicurist takes Claire's hand back, promising that it can be repaired quickly.

I roll my eyes and hold the phone up to her ear.

"J-Bear?" she says, then smiles at his reply while I do my best to mask my horrified expression at the sound of her pet name. "Hi, J-Bear. Yeah. I wanted to remind you that Mackenzie is allergic to mushrooms. Can you triple *triple* check that the caterer hasn't put mushroom anything in the baskets for the picnic?" She makes cooing noises at whatever he says. Then they have an entire conversation about whether he should come have his eyebrows waxed this afternoon, all while I'm holding the phone. Surely her other hand must be dry by now. But she keeps talking while the others get up and head toward the front to pay, and finally, she winds up with a round of "I love you. Yes I do. I'll see you soon, J-Bear. I love you," before she smiles and nods, which I guess is my signal that I can hang up.

"Thanks," she says. "You're always such a big help."

I can't tell if she's being serious or not, so I follow the others out of the spa without replying.

As soon as we're clear and headed toward the lobby, I grab hold of Piper.

"Time to pay up," I say.

She laughs and trips after me, but Claire says, "Where are you going?"

For a second, Piper and I stare at each other, looking like a pair of teenagers caught sneaking in after curfew . . . or maybe sneaking out.

"Piper forgot something in her room," I say.

"But what about the picnic?"

If she knows what we're doing, I appreciate her estimate of how long we might take. But Piper shakes her head and says, "We'll be a few minutes behind you. I've got a rental car."

"Not like we can all fit in your car, anyway," I say, trying to sound like this has been the plan the whole time.

"It's my other glasses," Piper says, pushing the rainbow ones she's wearing up on her nose. "These ones are new, and they're giving me a headache."

Claire glances back and forth between us like she's debating on calling bullshit. She stares at Piper for a particularly long time. Maybe she's considering Piper's glasses. Between these and the blue ones from last night, I'm surprised Claire hasn't pitched a fit about either. We were told we were only allowed to wear gold accessories for the wedding, and Piper's obvious preference for bright colors violates that rule.

Finally, though, Claire says, "Okay. See you soon."

I exhale as she turns her back. My skin prickles in anticipation. We're ten steps from the elevator. If you include the ride upstairs, I'm maybe a minute from getting my hands on Piper, and it's—

"Kate. There you are."

My mom is hurrying across the lobby. Dad is following after her at a more bemused pace.

"Oh no," I say.

"Kate. We have a problem."

"Is this about Aunt Lynette?" I say. "Because the wedding is tomorrow. Even if you left for Switzerland right now—"

She waves me off impatiently. "No one is going to Switzerland. It's not about Lynette. She'll have to live with the disappointment of missing the wedding."

"Better than the disappointment of missing her child's birth," Dad says, but Mom doesn't respond. They've perfected the art of ignoring each other's snarky asides when it suits them, and Mom clearly has much bigger fish to fry.

"It's Grandma," she says.

I immediately go on alert. "Is she okay?" Grandma is in her eighties. She's got bad knees and her eyesight isn't what it used to be. There was a lot of angst about whether or not she should even fly out to Colorado for the wedding, but she'd insisted she was fine.

"Of course I'm going," she said. "It's been such a long time since there was a wedding in the family." That second part was almost definitely a dig at me. Most of my family has decided to operate on the out of sight, out of mind approach. We never talk about it. Any of it. The past or the present. But Grandma pestered me for months after the breakup, wanting to know what I'd done or hadn't done that had driven Jono away. The truth is, I still don't know. It wasn't any particular thing. No one cheated or lied. But one afternoon, he sat me down at the edge of our bed and said, "This isn't working anymore."

"She's fine," Mom says, then frowns as she reconsiders. "Well, not fine. She forgot to pack her shoes."

Oh no.

"Of course she has shoes," I say. Has Mom already forgotten about the debacle at airport security where she refused to take them off? Because I heard all about it after the fact, and the retelling was so vivid, it was like I was there.

"Her good shoes," Dad says wearily. He's got his hands in his pockets, and he looks like he's been through this conversation a few times already this morning.

"The ones she wants to wear tomorrow," Mom says. "She didn't put them in her suitcase."

"So she can wear the ones she has." Like many women her age, my grandmother basically lives in leather orthopedic shoes. I can't remember her ever wearing anything more athletic than a loafer.

Dad makes a noise that says my suggestion is the wrong one, and Mom buries her face in her hands.

"Or not?" I say.

"She needs to go to Harwood and buy something new."

Excuse me?

"That's forty-five minutes away. There isn't a single shoe store closer than that?"

"No one here carries her size," Mom says. "The closest place that might is in Harwood."

I groan. The saga of Grandma's feet will be told for generations. She's a size five extra wide with a narrow heel. I don't even know what that means, but any time she decides she needs new shoes, the shopping expedition is an odyssey that leaves a trail of tears in its wake. She's so well known in her neighborhood that I've seen salespeople flee before we get through the door.

"Okay, so you want me to cover for you at the picnic?" I ask. There's some irony here. Half the time, I feel like the family is trying to cover for me, jumping on top of my perceived failings and transgressions before they reach their target. For me to be the one to smooth things over is a refreshing change of pace.

"No, I need you to take her shoe shopping," Mom says.

"Oh, for fuck's sake." The words are out of my mouth before I realize it.

"Katherine!" Mom sounds appalled.

"Why me?" I look to Dad for support, but he only shrugs. "Ask Aunt Lois. She's Grandma's daughter. Shouldn't it be her doing this?"

"She already helped me this morning with Aunt Lynette and the seating chart."

And somehow driving an hour and a half with Grandma and traumatizing unwitting retail workers is my penance at the altar of Claire and Jono's happy ending?

"Why aren't you going, then?" I ask, but I know I've already lost.

Mom puts an affronted palm to her chest. "I'm the mother of the bride. I have to go to the picnic."

But the bride's older sister is expendable?

"Honey," Dad says. "You know your grandmother wants to look her best tomorrow."

"I'll go with you," Piper says suddenly. I swing around so fast that something in my neck pinches.

"No, Piper," Mom says. "That's so thoughtful of you. But you're a bridesmaid. You need to be at the picnic."

"I'm a bridesmaid," I say. Mom doesn't reply to that.

Piper says, "Someone should go with Kate. The roads up here are narrow and twisty. Having an extra set of eyes for random mountain goats running across the road isn't a bad idea."

Mom smiles at Piper like she hung the moon.

"That's so sweet of you. Looking out for my girl."

"Claire will be pissed," I say. "She wants all her brides-maids at every event."

Piper gives me a sympathetic smile as she pushes up her glasses with her knuckles. "We'll be quick. Besides, I like your grandma. She's hilarious."

She's something.

"Great. Fine," I say. "Let's go."

Time to take a Colorado road trip with my crush and my grandma. Fun times.

5

"Are you sure they're not pinching? I think they're pinching." Grandma takes another slow walk in a circle, staring down at the navy blue pumps she's tried on four times already.

"They're the widest pair we have," the sales guy says. He sounds absolutely broken. A stack of boxes teeters beside his shoulder, ready to crush him like an avalanche. I swear we've tried on twenty pairs of shoes in the last hour. Half were dismissed immediately, but she narrowed it down to four different navy pumps and can't seem to make a decision.

"Grandma, why don't you wear the shoes you have?" I ask, and the sales guy throws me a grateful look.

"Those old things?" Her horrified look is a mirror of the one Mom uses for most of her so-called big crises. "There's no arch support. They hurt my bunions. How am I supposed to dance in those?"

I'm not sure how Grandma thinks she's going to dance in anything. She needed to get one of those golf carts with the flashing lights to make it through the airport. I don't begrudge her the support at all, but I can't see how that's going to translate to cutting a rug tomorrow night.

"What about these?" Piper holds up a pair of shoes that went into the reject pile almost immediately back when we first started. They're green patent leather with a gold buckle over the toe. They look like they were fashionable about forty years ago. Honestly, they'd go great with Piper's pedal pushers and cardigan.

I expect Grandma to turn up her nose again, but instead she says, "Oh, Piper, sweetheart. Those are perfect. Where did you find them?"

I throw up my arms, and the sales guy looks like he might cry. But Grandma takes the shoes from Piper like an octogenarian fairy-tale princess. We all hold our collective breaths as she slides them on and takes a few tentative steps, pausing in front of the mirror to examine the way they look on her. I made the mistake of telling her the first couple pairs look great on her, which only made Grandma sniff and tell the sales guy they were too small, so now I hold my tongue and let her come to her own conclusions.

"These might be all right," she says, and I nearly fall over with shock. Until she asks, "Do you have them in blue?"

We all groan and slump back down.

Twenty-five minutes later, we leave with the green shoes. I'd say it's only fifty-fifty that she'll actually wear them tomorrow, but I have done my duty.

"Looks like we're missing the picnic," I mutter to Piper as we get back in the rental car.

"I didn't want to go on the damn picnic anyway," Grandma says, sliding into the backseat. "Those llamas are disgusting. They spit, you know."

"Grandma, they're alpacas," I say, putting the car in gear. "And I'm sure they're very sweet. They wouldn't let tourists take out a bunch of grumpy alpacas."

Grandma pouts, looking out the window, as I pull us out of our parking spot. The drive was closer to an hour than forty-five minutes, which means we've already been gone for close to three hours. The picnic is long gone. I'll be lucky to have time to shower before the rehearsal dinner.

"Katherine, I'm hungry. We didn't stop for lunch."

So close.

"Grandma, we have to get going. Can you wait for dinner?"

"Absolutely not." She sounds scandalized. "What about my blood sugar?"

To the best of my knowledge, Grandma is not diabetic. No reason to worry about her blood sugar more than anyone else's.

"We can stop at a drive-through," I say. "I hope you like burgers."

"Well, I need to use the restroom," she says.

We stop for fast food, leaving Grandma at the front door to go use the facilities while Piper and I circle around for the drive-through. We could all go inside, I guess, but I refuse to leave the car. It's the principle of the thing. We order fries, a couple of burgers, and some chicken nuggets in case Grandma changes her order in the time she's inside the restaurant. I ask for a root beer and Piper gets a strawberry milkshake. By the time we pick up the order, Grandma's still not back, so I pull into a parking spot facing the door so we can see her come out.

"Cheers," I say, lifting my cup toward hers.

Piper arches an eyebrow, but instead of knocking her milkshake against my drink, she leans over the console and kisses me. Her lips are cold and sweet, making me shiver.

"I was falling behind," she says. "First the manicure, now this."

"Pretty sure this"—I gesture around us—"needs more than a milkshake-flavored kiss."

She unbuttons the top of her shirt, just enough to reveal the cleavage hiding underneath.

"Better?" she asks.

Is it? I can't tell. I definitely want to keep kissing her, but sometimes looking at her body like this feels wrong. She's still Piper. Little Piper.

Before I can ask her when she stopped being the little girl who wanted to tell me about her rock collection, a shadow passes over her face as Grandma comes around the car and climbs back into the backseat. I hand her a box of chicken nuggets, which she sneers at for a moment, but they, along with the accompanying french fries, have been entirely consumed by the time we hit the highway. As we pass the sign that says we have thirty miles to go, she's snoring softly, her head tilted back and her mouth open.

Piper smiles softly as she watches Grandma in the rearview mirror.

"They grow up so fast," she says.

"They certainly do." I give her what I hope is a lecherous grin, and she blows me a kiss. Unfortunately, that's all we can do, what with me driving and my grandma in the backseat.

"So . . ." Piper says, chewing on the word like she can't quite figure out the next one. "What's up with the dead people?"

Yeesh. I haven't had to answer that one in a while. In Albany, the people I know are all from my program. And my parents and I have silently agreed it's better not to talk about it, because it inevitably leads to questions about why I don't go back to med school.

"It's important," I say. "I want to help people."

"And you couldn't do that as a doctor?" She laughs, then realizes that I'm not joining her and bites her lip. "Sorry."

"Not the same. So much of medicine is so impersonal." Over the course of my studies, I met so many doctors who didn't see their patients as people anymore, just a list of symptoms. I didn't ever want to become that jaded. "People are afraid of death, but it's often when loved ones need the most support."

Last fall, in the first semester of the program, we'd had a bunch of guest speakers who had come in to tell us what it was like working in a funeral home. Some had really awful stories about family drama or funerals where no one showed up. Others had really sweet memories of people they built relationships with through the preplanning process. But everywhere there were stories of people feeling alone and needing a shoulder to cry on or someone to tell them the honest truth. I know something about feeling alone when life rocks you; it's not quite the same as a family member dying, but I did my fair share of grieving while I was traveling.

Piper doesn't say anything else about my career choice. Most people don't. It's fine.

But since she's opened the door, I might as well step through it and make good on getting to know her a little better instead of spending all my time trying to better acquaint myself with that little red bra.

"What about you?" I ask. "I don't even know where you're living now."

She arches an eyebrow. "Didn't think to ask at the party last year, did you?"

I gape. "Well, I—I thought—I wasn't—"

Piper reaches over the console to shove at my shoulder, hard enough to make me sway, but not so hard I have to take my eyes off the road.

"I live in Vermont," she says. "White River Junction."

I whistle. "That's a long way from Westchester."

She shrugs. "Less than four hours if you don't hit weekend traffic."

"You know what I mean." It's New England. Nothing is that far. But Jono's family had a winter place up in Vermont. It's pretty if you don't mind trees and every other car being a Subaru, but it's not exactly metropolitan.

Another shrug. "I moved up there with someone after college."

"With someone?" I ask, leering. "Or *someone*?"

Piper wrinkles her nose, and I feel bad making her uncomfortable when I'm only trying to kill time as we go back up the valley road.

"It didn't work out. She moved back home, and I stayed. The people are nice, rent is cheap, and I can do my job from anywhere."

"What is it you do again?" Claire and her friends all work for tech and design companies.

"I'm an outdoor sports social media influencer."

"Oh." I try to picture Piper in her polka dots and plaid smiling up at the phone on her selfie stick, telling adoring fans about living her best blessed life.

She bursts out laughing. "I'm kidding. I mean, you can't live in Vermont and not enjoy spending time outside, but I actually own my own business. I make jewelry."

I risk a glance at her. She's wearing a pair of pearl studs in her ears. "Like those?"

"No." She touches the small round circle. "These were my grandmother's. I don't work in gold, so I didn't bring anything this weekend."

"But you make a living?" God, I sound like my mom. *How are you going to make a living, Katherine? You'd be making so much more as a doctor, Katherine.* She only calls me Katherine when she's angry or feels especially ignored.

I would make more money as a doctor, but I'd hate it. The more I traveled, the farther I walked from my old life, the more I knew that was the truth. I'd originally pitched the backpacking trip to my parents as a hiatus. I was three years into med school and needed a semester off to get my head back in the game. Jono and I had always talked about hiking the Appalachian trail, and I decided to do it solo instead. But two weeks out, I knew I wasn't going back to med school . . . and that I wasn't going to finish the trail either. There was too much else out there. Too much to see after a lifetime of staying on one path. Undergrad, then med school, then a successful career in a hospital somewhere. Jono and only Jono, until we were old and gray.

Piper doesn't seem put off by my question, though. "I do okay. I had a couple social media posts go viral last year. My ear cuff got picked up by some socialites in Tribeca and a model in LA. Things got busy for a while after that."

"But not anymore?"

She lowers the visor and checks her makeup in the mirror. Honestly, her face is perfect. Red lips, jet-black mascara. She knows how to wear it. I used to think I had some kind of personality flaw that left me unable to confidently apply makeup, but I've concluded it's not part of my identity. It's part of Piper's, though, and she's clearly taken the time to learn how to do it well.

"I'm waiting for new inspiration to hit," she says. "I have to change up my line about every six months or it gets stale. I'm doing a new store drop next month. I'll send you a link if you want to get on the advance sales list."

"Aww. You'd do that for me?" Jewelry's not really my thing. It's frowned on at school. Nothing like losing a bracelet or one of Grandma's pearl earrings in a chest cavity to really spoil the day. And while I was traveling, it was one more thing to lose or have stolen or rub against your skin until you develop a weird rash. But I'd be happy to check out Piper's work.

Behind us, Grandma snorts and starts.

"You're not getting my pearls. Don't even think about it," she says. Sleep talking runs in our family, apparently. Piper gives her a quirky glance in the mirror before she puts the visor back up, and Grandma drifts off like nothing happened.

I don't want her pearls, anyway. See the aforementioned body cavity problem.

I'd take Piper's, though. Or her earlobe. Between my teeth, hard enough to make her moan.

I step on the gas.

"Something wrong?" Piper asks.

"We're running out of time," I say.

"For what?" But her tone says she knows exactly what. She settles back on her seat. "Better get going, then."

Oh, we are.

6

We are not.

It's inevitable, perhaps, though it's starting to feel like my family is conspiring against me. We pull into the lodge around three-thirty. Our next official activity isn't until six. Lots of time for Piper and I to get to know each other a little bit better. Finally.

"Come on, Grandma," I say, practically pulling her from the car in the lodge parking lot. "You look tired. I think you need a nap."

"I slept all the way back into town," she grumbles, and yanks her elbow free. I'm not prepared for how strong she is, and I overbalance. It's only Piper standing behind me that keeps me from crashing to the pavement. Grandma glares at me before she strides toward the front door.

The front door where Aunt Lois is now striding out to meet us with a look of worry on her face and—

"Is that blood on your shirt?" I ask.

"What?" She rubs at the reddish-brown stain on her sunshine yellow sweater. "Oh, darn. I thought it missed me."

"What missed you? Are you okay?"

"I'm fine." She waves me off. "Hi, Mom. Did you find your shoes?"

"Katherine wouldn't let us stop for a proper lunch," Grandma says by way of answer. "I had to eat processed chicken feet and corn starch masquerading as potatoes. The food at the dinner tonight better be an improvement. What about my blood sugar?"

"Grandma, there's nothing wrong with your blood sugar," I say, but she ignores me, shuffling toward the front door. Lois is hovering at her elbow and looks far more nervous than I'm used to seeing her. Normally, she's the world-weary older sister and Mom's the one teetering on the edge of a breakdown.

"Lois," I say, hurrying to catch up. Piper's behind me, clutching the bag with Grandma's shoes in them. "What's going on? Did something happen at the picnic?"

"Oh." Lois stops short, smacking her forehead like she can't believe she forgot something. There's another rusty stain on the underside of her sleeve. "Kate, your sister's in the hospital."

"What?" Piper and I both say at the same time.

"It was the alpacas," Lois said, shaking her head. Grandma's still making a beeline for the lodge, like Claire's fate is of no concern to her.

"What about the alpacas?" I ask.

"They got loose. We had such a nice lunch too. The views were so pretty, and there were these little smoked salmon roll-ups with this dill cream cheese wrapped up in—"

"Lois!" I clap my hands right in front of her face. "Focus. Claire. Hospital. Rogue alpacas." I've never seen an alpaca up close, but I've seen them online, and honestly, they seem so cute and fluffy. If Claire has met a tragic end in an alpaca-related incident the day before her wedding, I hope it was the most adorable trampling ever.

"Right," Lois says. "So we were halfway back to the picnic site and one of them got spooked. I don't know what for. Maybe a fly or a snake. Do they have snakes up here at this time of year?"

"Lois," I say again. If she takes much longer, I'll get in the rental and drive right down to the hospital myself.

"Anyway, one of them got scared. And another started to jump around. And then a third took off, and Claire got dragged along—"

"Dragged along?" Suddenly, my imagined trampling isn't so cute.

"Well, she was leading it back from the picnic, and when it started to run, she didn't let go right away, and . . ." She shrugs, and I really can't see why she's so unruffled by the whole thing. I spin on my heel. "Where are you going?"

"To the hospital," I say, rushing back to the rental.

"I'll go with you," Piper says.

"No, it's fine." I don't need the distraction.

"She's my friend."

"Piper!" Madison and the other bridesmaids are coming out of the lodge. Was everyone waiting for us to return so they could ambush us in the parking lot? "There's a problem with the centerpieces at the rehearsal tonight."

"Go," I tell her. "I'll text you when I know more."

As it turns out, the town does not have a hospital. I drive around in circles for twenty minutes before I finally have to stop and look up the closest one on my phone. It's back in Harwood, not far from the shoe store, actually. The idea of driving there again makes me groan. But the second search result that comes up is for a clinic in town that says it offers urgent care, so I follow the map instructions and find it on a quiet side street. There are six cars parked out front, including Jono's obnoxious green convertible, so at least I know I'm in the right place.

"Oh, Katie!" My mom practically hurls herself in my arms sobbing as I walk into the waiting room.

"What? What's wrong? Is Claire okay?"

But she keeps weeping. She's making unintelligible sounds that might be words, but if they are, I don't speak that language.

"She's fine," Dad says, coming out of an exam room. There's dirt on his shirt and the jacket he's wearing has a small tear in the sleeve, but otherwise, he appears unhurt.

"She's not fine!" Mom pulls herself together long enough to howl at my dad. She came at me so fast that I didn't get a chance to really look at her before. Her face is puffy from crying and there's a grass stain on one of her knees, but she also seems no worse for wear. "She's getting married tomorrow, David, and now she's . . ." The words get weepy again, but at least this time she folds herself against my dad, who patiently pats her hair.

"A few scratches and bruises," Dad says to me. "Your friends will have to get creative with some makeup for the scrape on her arm tomorrow, but other than that—"

"She's wounded!" Mom says.

"She has a small cut on her forehead," Dad says. "The doctor says she'll need stitches, but then she'll be all set."

Mom disagrees, though the grounds for her objection are vague and said entirely into Dad's chest. He keeps murmuring appeasements, and I'm left there standing by myself. Maybe I shouldn't have come. Stitches aren't the end of the world. When I was eight and Claire was four, we were skating, and I slipped and put a tooth through my lower lip. I needed two stitches to hold it together, and that moment was memorialized in all our family Christmas photos that year. But despite the trauma, I turned out okay. Mostly.

Mom's calming down and Dad's talking about concussions and whether or not Claire can drink at the rehearsal or at the reception tomorrow night, and I realize an important person is missing from the room.

"Where's Jono?" I ask. Mom and Dad get quiet and give each other guilty glances, making my pulse pick up again.

"He's down the hall," Dad says. "Lying down."

"Lying down? Why?"

Mom puts a hand on my arm, steering me toward that same hall. "Go check on him. He'd probably like to see a friendly face."

I try to wrestle clear, but Mom's staring at me with a cultish kind of intensity that makes me even more uncomfortable than going to check on Jono, so I finally relent and hurry away from her.

The door to the exam room is open, and Jono is lying on the paper-covered table inside. Out of everyone, he looks to be in the best shape. No blood, no dirt. His shirt is untucked, but otherwise, he looks fine. Maybe a little pale.

I knock on the doorframe, and he rolls his head toward me. His smile is slow and guilty, though I'm sure that guilt has nothing to do with me.

"Mom wanted me to ask if you're okay?" I say, because saying I wanted to know if he was okay feels risky.

He runs a hand over his face, then sits up slowly, swinging his legs over the side.

"I'm fine," he says, voice rough. "Sorry. I didn't mean to scare anyone."

"While you were running for your life from a homicidal alpaca?" I ask.

"Fucking alpacas." He shakes his head. "They were Claire's idea. She said it would make for great pictures. They didn't see it that way."

The room settles into silence. It's the two of us, and

suddenly that feels like one too many. I say, "Okay, well, we'll see you out in the waiting room. Let me know if you can drive back safely."

"Do you remember," he asks as I turn back toward the hall, and he pauses, waiting until I turn back around to continue, "that time we were hiking near Storm King Mountain?"

I close my eyes, trying not to remember. We'd been studying for finals at the end of our second year of med school. We hadn't seen daylight or breathed fresh air in four days, and on that morning, we'd finally run out of coffee to keep us going. Jono had said we were going to buy more, but then he kept driving, right out of the city and north up the Hudson Valley. It was spring and the ground was barely melted, but that also meant we had the whole place to ourselves. At the time, it felt like the perfect kind of day, and one I tried to recreate a lot while I was traveling alone. I always looked for spots the tourists wouldn't be, asking locals and spending hours on the internet to find hidden gems.

That day at Storm King was perfect. Except for—

I put my hands over my mouth. "Oh no."

The perfection lasted until we were almost all the way down. Seriously, we could see the car in the parking lot. Then, out of nowhere, we were attacked.

The vengeful Canada goose can be a popular meme on social media, but you haven't felt true fear until one is hissing and nipping at your heels as you sprint the last fifty yards off the side of a mountain to your rusting Ford Fiesta. To this day, I still don't know where it came from or what we did to enrage it, but one minute I was feeling like maybe we would survive our finals after all, and the next I was sure we weren't even going to make it back to the city, much less to the exam.

I giggle, eyes going wide when I inadvertently snort. Jonathan's grinning too.

"I've never been so afraid in my life," I say.

"I can still hear you screaming. 'Faster! Faster!'" His voice goes high.

My mouth drops open. "I don't sound like that."

"You definitely did."

"No, I didn't." But I'm still laughing. For a minute, everything feels . . . well, not exactly normal. It's been such a long time since I've been alone with him or said more than a few words to him that I can't really say what normal is between me and Jonathan anymore. But it feels relaxed, and that's pretty good too.

I take a chance to look at him. *Really* look at him. I've done my best to avoid him since we arrived in Colorado, just like I did when he and Claire stopped by Mom and Dad's at Christmas last year. And before that, the only other time I've seen him was at the engagement party, where I spent most of my time locked away with Piper. I can't say he's changed. It hasn't been that long since I saw his face every day. A few years, not decades. His hair is shorter but still a dull mousey brown. There's a small round mark on his cheek that might be a new scar but might also be a pimple that's not fully healed yet. Even though I met him in undergrad, Jono still had acne that would make a teenager blush. It cleared up by the end of our sophomore year, but he's still prone to breakouts, or he was when we were engaged. Does Claire know that? Does she know the type of tea tree oil he likes to manage spots when they rear their ugly heads?

But it doesn't matter if she does or not. It's not my business to ask.

He says, "Are you okay, Katie?" and my laughter dies. My gaze drops to my shoes.

"I'm fine. I'm not the one who nearly got run over by an

alpaca. I should be making sure you're okay. Is the doctor coming to check you out when Claire's stitches are done?"

"What? No, I'm fine." He looks flustered. "I wasn't anywhere near the alpaca when it—I was helping my mom. She's in a walking cast after she sprained her ankle playing tennis a couple of weeks ago and wasn't feeling very steady on the path back to the car and—"

"Wait." I hold up a hand. "You weren't part of the alpacapocalypse?"

He grins but shakes his head. "I wish. If I'd been closer, I might have been able to get Claire to let go of that lead rope faster."

"Then what are you doing here?" I gesture at the exam room.

He flushes, and now it's his turn to look at his shoes. He bangs them gently against the table, twisting his fingers in his lap as he says, "Claire wanted me in there while they did the sutures. But the second they put the needle in her forehead for the anesthetic, I went a bit . . ." He wobbles where he's sitting, and his expression is sheepish when he glances up at me.

I gasp. "You fainted?"

"I didn't faint." His tone is indignant. "The room got a little spinny, and—"

"Jono, you're a doctor! You can't faint at the sight of needles." I'm laughing again.

"I said I didn't faint. And I don't do it when I'm the one using the needle. But it was different because it was Claire and there was a lot of blood and . . ." He trails off with a sigh.

What a weekend. I'm sorry I missed the alpaca adventure, but I'm not going to make him feel bad for how he reacted here. Lots of people do it. I had a classmate who fainted two hours into an anatomy lab. We were elbow deep in a cadaver and he'd been fine, but then he looked down and realized the thing he'd thought was a footrest beneath his shoes was actually an arm in a bag, and that was it. Lights out. You never know how you're going to react until you're in that very specific arm-in-a-bag situation.

"Kate?" My dad's coming up the hall behind me. "Claire's done. Is Jonathan doing better?"

Jono hops off the table steadily enough that I'm not concerned.

"I'm fine, David," he says.

"That's good. How about you, Kate?" Dad slings an arm around my shoulder, which prevents me from making a quick escape as Jono comes toward the door. "You doing okay?"

I freeze. It's the question I've most wanted to hear, but it's still not right. He wants to know if I have some sort of secondary trauma or survivor's guilt since I wasn't part of the alpaca nightmare. Nothing deeper than that.

"Grandma's going to say I wouldn't let her eat and she nearly lapsed into a diabetic coma on the way back," I say, and even Jonathan groans.

"She made me look at the notes from her last doctor's visit yesterday," he says. "She literally brought printouts of the test results in her luggage. I promised her there was nothing wrong with her bloodwork. She'll outlive us all running purely on spite."

Dad chuckles. "Hopefully you didn't say that last part to her."

"Why would I do that? I want to live long enough to get married tomorrow."

His words should make me angry. Or sad. But as we walk down the hall, I prod at my feelings, looking for signs of injury. Not much there. Old wounds, mostly healed over. Thick scar tissue that makes their range of motion a little less than it used to be. I wasn't lying when I told Piper I'm not in love with Jono anymore.

"Oh, J-Bear!" Claire barrels out of her exam room, nearly knocking a nurse over, and hurls herself into Jono's arms, much the way my mom did when I walked into the clinic. From what I can see, there's a red scrape on her forearm, and when she lifts her head from his shoulder, a white square of bandage taped to her forehead becomes visible. Her bangs are crusted together, dark red-brown where the rest of her hair is still the blonde we both had as kids. She swipes at her eyes as she looks over Jono's shoulder at me.

"What are you doing here?"

"I—" The explanation eludes me. Aunt Lois said Claire was hurt, and my only thought was to leap in the car and make sure she was okay. But now that I'm here and she's got Jono's arms wrapped around her, I wonder if I shouldn't have come.

"I don't want anyone seeing me like this." She cowers behind Jono's frame. "I'm getting married tomorrow."

"Oh, come on, Claire." I try to keep my tone light. "It's not that bad."

"Get out," she says, clearly channeling Mom as she points imperiously toward the door.

"Claire," Dad says.

"It's fine," I say, taking an unsteady step back. I shouldn't have stuck my nose into this. "I'll go back to the hotel. See you all at dinner."

I'm not in love with Jono anymore, but that doesn't mean there isn't still some healing to do.

7

For once, there's no one waiting to deliver bad news or issue edicts as I walk across the hotel lobby. In fact, I feel downright invisible, which is ideal, really. I make my way up to my room, already dreading the rehearsal dinner. If Claire didn't want me seeing her at the clinic, she's not going to want a larger group seeing her with that bandage on her head. I'm already imagining Jono tenderly washing the blood out of her bangs and then Claire taking a full hour with an arsenal of curling irons and hair products to find a way to try and mask whatever injury lies beneath.

Guess that leaves me time to try and finish writing my speech.

When I get back up to my room, there's a note slid under the door. Claire or one of the bridesmaids has clearly asked the hotel to let everyone know the dinner is going to be delayed. A second note from Aunt Lois says she's gone into town for a massage. Honestly, that sounds heavenly. I roll my head on my shoulders, trying to work out the knots, but there's only so much I can do on my own. I take a shower instead, letting the hot water do its thing, which helps a little, and mentally go over my talking points for the speech I still haven't written.

Ever since she was little, Claire always knew ...

The first time I met Jono, he was ...

Love is patient, love is kind ...

Bullshit.

None of it sounds sincere or profound in any way. And maybe that's the point. Speeches at weddings are always unapologetically optimistic. They're a spoken-word version of a Live-Laugh-Love wall hanging. At Claire's bridal shower, there was a guestbook where the old married ladies were supposed to leave their secret for a long marriage, and at least half of them wrote "never go to bed angry." How is that possible over the course of an entire married life? Don't go to bed pissed off that Jono has that one snarly toenail he insists on cutting in the den while you're trying to watch TV, sure, but it's going to happen at least once that one person in the relationship will do something egregious enough that they both go to sleep upset. Pretending it doesn't happen is the worst kind of toxic positivity bullshit.

Yeah, none of that can go in my speech. No one would believe me, anyway. I'm the burnout older sister who got her heart broken, quit her fast track to a successful adulthood, and fled the country.

Love is patient, love is kind. Jono and Claire were made for each other.

I stare at my clothes hanging in the closet. The pink monstrosity stares back. Not like I have options to pick from for tonight. I packed a black jumpsuit I bought in Prague and never found a reason to wear. It's basically a mile of pleated crepe that feels like I'm wearing nothing, and I know I look amazing in it. I've never had much in the way of hips or curves, but the halter neck and low back show off my good features. It's my version of a revenge dress, though I'm not really sure who I'm getting revenge on anymore.

Still . . . the effect, once I've slapped on a little lipstick and some earrings—silver hoops because Claire doesn't get to dictate my jewelry until tomorrow—is impressive, if I do say so myself. At least I don't look like I got run down by an alpaca today.

A gentle knock comes on my door. My whole body goes heavy with the idea of facing whatever family member waits on the other side. I've done my duties today. All that's left for me to do is get through this dinner in one piece and—

"Hey, I wanted to see if you were ready, and—" Piper's talking as I open the door, but as I step fully into the doorway, she trails off. She does a full-body up and down, and when her gaze lands on mine, whatever she was going to say is gone and replaced with the purest speculative heat. She bites her lip—still perfectly red—and says, "Holy shit, Katie."

"Holy shit yourself," I say, and I'm not exaggerating. Her dress is black lace with an oyster-colored lining. Her waist is cinched with a silver belt and flares into a crinoline-poofy skirt with a scalloped edge. The plunging neckline frames her cleavage perfectly and is so wide that it looks like it's barely clinging to her shoulders. She stands on pencil-thin patent leather stilettos that would kill me within seconds of putting them on, but she doesn't even wobble.

We stare for a long time, like we're each standing on opposite edges of a canyon trying to figure out how to cross.

"Your aunt?" Piper asks, voice breathy.

"Not here," I say.

That's all she needs to know. Whether she rushes forward or I pull her into the room is unclear and irrelevant. The point is, the door swings shut behind us, and for the first time we are—oh finally, thank God, finally—alone.

For a second, we hover, inches apart. My fingers are splayed wide at my sides, unsure of where I can and can't touch her. Her eyes roam my face and my body.

"Still a bad idea?" she asks, making me cringe.

"Not in the slightest. You weren't then, and you definitely aren't now."

She twitches, like she's still trying to hold back. "I'm afraid I'll wrinkle something. You look so pretty."

I'm not sure this fabric wrinkles, but I appreciate her consideration. Without hesitating, I reach behind my neck to the clasp and pull it free. The fabric falls easily, sliding over my skin with a hiss until I'm naked from the waist up. I'm not wearing a bra, and my nipples go hard as the cool air from the air-conditioned room hits them.

"There you go," I say. "A hundred percent wrinkle-proof. At least for a few more years."

Bullseye. Piper finally reaches for me, pulling me to her, crushing the stiff crinoline between us. The lace is gently rough against my bare skin, as are her lips against mine. I've been waiting to do this all day, and now that it's finally happening, I'm starving for it.

She steps out of her heels, which I'm a little sad about, but I quickly forget that small stab of disappointment as she backs me up, kissing me the whole time. My knees hit the bed, and I sink down, wrapping my arms around her waist so she has to come with me. She straddles my hips, still kissing. Her fingers brush over the short strands at the back of my neck, and I mouth over her chest and along her collarbones.

"Kate," she says.

"We don't have a lot of time," I say. I bunch the stiff fabric of her skirt up in my hands until I find her thighs. They're smooth and warm, and she thumbs my nipples as I explore, finding the thin line of her underwear beneath her hip bones and following it back to where they meet below the small of her back and travel downward as a thong.

"Jesus, Piper, where did you learn to dress like this?"

Her smile as she looks down at me is all warm pride.

"Do you like it?" she asks, and for a second I can hear the kid I knew. The one who would greet me when I came home from band practice or wherever to find her and Claire on the couch watching TV. The way she wrinkles her nose is the same way she used to do it while she sat at my parents' table and laughed over pizza.

"It's like you were made for it," I say. I let go of her thighs and run my hands over her torso. Unlike me, she's got some serious hardware going on under there. "Are you wearing the corset again?"

"A different one," she says. "I'll show you later, if you like."

I want to ask why not now, but before I can, she pinches the nipple she's been playing with. I gasp, then go weak as she pushes me down onto the mattress so she can lie alongside me, running her tongue over the same spot she just pinched. The lingering sting and the warm wetness are amazing. I lift one foot off the ground and brace it on the edge of the mattress, letting the soft pleated fabric swish against my skin. It wouldn't take much to wriggle out of it. Or guide one of Piper's hands underneath it. I'm already wet, and if she would only touch me . . .

The whir of the lock is the only warning we get before the front door swings open. Piper leaps off me like an electrified cat, and maybe it was a good idea she took her shoes off, after all, because I don't know that anyone could stick the landing in those things, and we don't need another trip back to the town clinic. I hurry to stand too, and as Aunt Lois enters the room, we've both got our backs to the door while Piper helps me do up the jumpsuit again.

"Oh," I say, glancing over my shoulder like this is the most innocent and casual place to be in the entire hotel. "You're back. How was the massage? Piper was helping me finish getting ready."

Aunt Lois stops just inside the room. She glances between us, then toward the window, then over to my bed. The cover is slightly wrinkled, but we hadn't gotten far enough along for it to look suspicious. I kick myself for my verbal vomit, though. The key to a convincing lie is not to overshare the details.

Her gaze drops to Piper's shoes on the floor, and she says, "The massage was nice. The masseuse was an old man from the Czech Republic whose definition of *medium pressure* meant I had to breathe through the pain as he proudly told me about the time his *deep pressure* made a bodybuilder cry."

That sounds . . . unpleasant. But Aunt Lois lets out a happy sigh and says she's going to take a shower. She gives Piper's stilettos one last glance but doesn't say anything as she disappears into the bathroom. We wait, lips pressed together to smother nervous giggles, until the water starts running, then I push Piper to the door, scooping up her shoes as we go, and hurry out into the hall.

Laughter bursts from us once we're free of the room. My hands shake as I cover my face.

"That was awful," I say.

"Not all of it." Piper gives me a wicked look as she steps back into the black patent leather.

I can't help myself as I step into her space to kiss her. I put my hands on her waist, feeling the boning of the corset underneath. She hums happily under my lips, but the heat is mostly gone. We're not about to start making out in the hotel hallway. Later, though . . . She offered to show me the corset later, and I'm definitely going to take her up on that as soon as our obligations for the night are over.

We go down to the lobby, but no one is around. Piper suggests we check on Claire, and I follow her back to the elevator, hesitant after my banishing at the clinic, but I also don't want to tell Piper about that, so what am I supposed to do? We stand shoulder to shoulder as we ride back up to the fourth floor. There's room enough to spread apart, but I can't make myself step away. As the elevator slows, the back of her hand brushes against mine, and I tangle my fingers with hers for a split second. She throws a quick smile my way, then walks out into the hall, leaving me to follow. Not that I'm complaining. It means I get to admire the swing of her hips and the smooth line of her legs as she makes her way down the hall. The dress is unlined in the back, showing me the outline of her corset and tiny glimpses of her skin above that. It's fastened with a line of miniscule buttons, and I imagine undoing them one by one so I can press kisses down her spine.

She glances over her shoulder at me, like she knows what I'm thinking.

"There's a zipper along the side seam," she says. "No way can I be bothered with all those buttons. As soon as I tried it on, I knew I'd have to put a zipper in."

My feet scuff on the carpet. "You made the dress?"

"I'm flattered you think I could, but no. I bought it at a vintage shop in Williamsburg. I just altered it." She runs a hand over her waist. "Even with the corset, the bodice was too snug."

Well, it's not anymore. It looks like it was made for her. And I want to peel her out of it, inch by inch.

We arrive at Claire's door in time to hear her shout inside.

"What was that?" Piper asks, and I'm already knocking.

"Claire? Claire? Are you okay?" If she's fallen or hurt herself further, my mom will have a fit.

"Who is it?" Her voice sounds far away as she calls out.

"It's Kate. And Piper." I knock again. "We heard a shout. What happened?"

There's a long pause, then footsteps come toward the door, and finally, Claire opens it. Her hair is a mess, and the bandage has come off, revealing an angry line of black stitches underneath. Her cheeks are flushed, and she's wearing an oversized Columbia University sweatshirt that I recognize from med school days. Must be Jono's.

"What's wrong?" Claire asks.

In fact, even as Claire does her best to fully stand in the doorway, Jono is clearly visible inside the room. He's sitting on the bed with his back to us, pulling a T-shirt over his head.

"We wanted to see if you needed anything before dinner," Piper says, but I can't take my eyes off Jono, which is why, when he stands, I get to see him do up the front of his pants.

Ah.

"I think they're okay," I say.

"Yes." Claire's smile doesn't overpower the embarrassed flush that creeps over her cheeks. "Yeah, totally fine. We were . . ." She glances over her shoulder at Jono.

"Yeah. Yeah. No worries, then," I say, tugging on Piper's sleeve. "With the head injury and everything, I thought that—"

"What? No." She flutters a hand over her forehead. "No. Jonathan was—We were—" Her expression is pained. I know exactly what they were doing. The guilty look Jono is giving me now is the same one I probably gave Aunt Lois not ten minutes ago.

"We should go," I say. "Don't want to be late for the

dinner. Though I guess since you're both—" I mean to say since they're both not ready, but all I can do is make a nasal grunting sound as I gesture toward the room. Claire flushes, then her face grows serious as she looks me up and down. Her brows pinch together, though one side doesn't move as far as the other because of her stitches, making her look lopsided.

"Is that what you're wearing to the rehearsal dinner?" she asks.

I freeze, running my hands over the pleats. The damn thing even has pockets, which I now shove my hands into, trying not to look self-conscious.

"You don't like it?" I ask.

She pinches her lips together, considering, and I clench my teeth.

"It's a bit severe, isn't it?" she asks Piper, who has the good grace to say nothing.

"Severe?" I say, pulling the material away from my legs so she can see the way it flows. Something this light can never be called severe.

"Well, it's black," she says, sounding exasperated.

"So is Piper's." I'm sorry to draw her into this, but the point stands. "Is she too severe?"

"No." Claire shakes her head. "Because it's Piper, and she's—"

"She's what?" My voice is rising.

"Shh, Kate. People will hear."

"I think you look great, Katie," Jono says as he comes to stand behind Claire.

"But it's black." Claire's whining now. "It's all black. She might as well be going to a funeral, not a wedding."

"The wedding isn't until tomorrow," I say.

"Piper's dress is black," Jono says, and I'm annoyed by both the fact that he said I look good and the fact that when he points out Claire's hypocrisy, she slumps, whereas when I did it, she doubled down.

"I didn't pack anything else," I say. "So it's either this or I'm back to jeans and flannel. Your choice."

What follows is a silent sisterly standoff. Our hair may not be the same color, but our eyes are the exact same shade of hazel, and we stare at each other wordlessly for a long time. I'm so over this weekend. I'm so over Claire's controlling bullshit. I'm here, aren't I? I'm putting on the happy face everyone expects. And frankly, I look hot in this jumpsuit. If Claire doesn't like it, she can go chase some alpacas.

Finally, Jono puts an arm around her waist and kisses her cheek. He murmurs something in her ear that makes her curl up around her smile, and there's a very good chance that as soon as we're gone, they'll be back to whatever it was they were doing before we knocked on the door.

She says, "That's fine, Katie. It's very nice. Tell Mom we're going to be a few minutes late for dinner."

I've been dismissed. I keep my mouth clamped shut, and Piper has to tell her we'll relay the message and see her at the restaurant. My spine feels like an iron post as we return to the elevator. At one point, Piper brushes her fingers over my exposed back, and I immediately regret wearing this ridiculous thing at all. But if I change into my other clothes, both Claire and Mom will freak out, so instead I'm stuck wearing a piece of clothing I felt incredibly desirable in only a few minutes ago and I'm now trapped in out of spite.

Once we're alone in the elevator, Piper softly says, "You're going to have to forgive her at some point."

I fold my arms over my chest. "She didn't say anything about what we were supposed to wear to dinner. I'm already wearing that horrible pink fashion crime tomorrow. I wanted to look good tonight."

"You look amazing," she says. "But that's not what I meant."

I know what she meant. She means that I have to forgive my sister for slipping into Jono's heart after he broke mine. And that would be the grown-up thing.

"In order for me to forgive her, she has to acknowledge that she did something shitty first," I say, then bite my lip, regretting my impulsiveness. I've never actually said the words out loud.

"It was hard for her," Piper says. "She felt super guilty when they first started seeing each other."

I scoff. "Yeah, I'm sure it was so hard for both of them."

Piper doesn't say anything else, which is for the best. Pleading Claire's case is not going to do her any favors. This isn't her battle to fight. The fact is that my fiancé dumped me and within two years, he'd not only started dating my little sister, but decided he wanted to marry her. And she never once told me any of it. Never once asked me how I felt about them being together.

I'm fighting tears by the time the elevator doors slide open. Mom and Dad and Aunt Lois and others are milling around, along with Madison and the rest of the bridal party.

"Did you see Claire?" she asks as I stride through the lobby, doing my best not to make eye contact.

"Kate, did you stop by Grandma's room?" Mom asks.

I ignore them. Piper makes some hasty replies. I get all the way to the rental car before I realize that if I drive off in a huff, Mom and Dad will have no way of getting to the restaurant.

Families are so goddamn messy.

I only need to spend another thirty-six hours with mine, and then I can put the space between them I so desperately need.

8

THANKS TO THE ALPACA AFTERMATH, WE DON'T ACTUALLY have a rehearsal, just a rehearsal dinner, which suits me fine. If anyone is confused by the idea of walking in a straight line down an aisle, we have bigger problems.

Dinner is at an Italian place in town that gives off cozy, relaxed vibes. No white linen tablecloths, but a decent step up from checkered vinyl and wine bottle candleholders covered in decades of wax. People arrive slowly, and a space has been set aside for us to mingle over drinks. Jono's parents, Ted and Adrian, are already there when Piper and I and my parents arrive.

"Oh, Katie. It's so good to see you." Adrian pulls me in for a tight hug. She's a broad woman whose specialty has always been rib-cracking bear hugs, and even though it's super awkward to be face-to-face with her after all this time, the embrace is a relief. I lean into it, wrapping my arms around her shoulders and squeezing her back for everything I'm worth.

"It's good to see you too," I say when she lets go enough that I can breathe again. "It's been a while."

Mom and Dad are talking with a server and getting

Grandma set up in a chair. Piper is chatting with one of the other bridesmaids. So it's just me and Jono's parents to speak to each other.

"We wanted to say something at the engagement party last year," Ted says. "But we didn't . . ." He shrugs.

I bite my lip. I've always loved Jono's parents. They welcomed me from the first time we met, and while people always warn you that getting married isn't only about choosing a spouse, it's about choosing an extended family too, I was never nervous about being part of Jono's family.

"How are you holding up?" Adrian gives my shoulder a sympathetic pat. Her palm is warm. "This whole weekend has to be hard for you. Honestly, Claire is wonderful, and they're both so happy, but we told them that this all seemed awfully fast, and—"

"It's fine," I say, because a minute ago all I wanted was sympathy, but now that it's in front of me, I can't accept it. It's not Ted and Adrian's fault. They're not responsible for or required to apologize for Jono's actions. "I'm glad they're happy together. Tomorrow is going to be a fun day."

They don't look convinced, even when I punctuate my platitudes with a smile. So I take the cheap way out and make a big fuss about Adrian's sprained ankle, which then follows with lots of questions about my travels, until we're all back on safe ground. The restaurant fills up with friends and family, and Claire and Jono arrive last to much applause and concerned questions about Claire's ordeal with the alpaca and whether she'll be able to make it down the aisle tomorrow under her own power. Considering she's practically glowing under all the attention, I'm sure she'll be fine for the ceremony. She's pinned her bangs in such a way the stitches are completely covered, and no doubt she'll look even better when she's in the capable hands of the stylist she's hired.

I keep a wide berth between me and the happy couple through the whole cocktail hour. There's no seating plan for dinner tonight, so I sit with Ted and Adrian and a couple of Jono's relatives. They all ask how I'm doing but don't dig any deeper when I say I'm okay and ask how they've been. If anyone thinks it's weird that I'm not sitting with my own family or the rest of the bridal party, no one says anything.

Dinner is tasty. Actually, the eggplant parm is to die for. As coffee and dessert are served, people start to mingle again, and the chair beside me frees up. Somewhere along the line, Piper slides into it. She looks like she might try to take my hand, so I busy myself stirring sugar into my coffee.

"You okay?" she asks.

"Fine." God, I hate that word. I've said it so much this weekend that it's lost all meaning. And I *am* fine. I'm not dying. Bleeding. I have money in the bank, and I'm training for a meaningful career. I've seen more of the world than most people ever will, and in just a few more hours, I'll be getting up close and personal with Piper's corset and what lies beneath. So really, fine.

Laughter goes up at the table behind us. Jono and a couple of groomsmen are clearly having a good time, with several empty wine glasses scattered on the table between them.

Piper waits for the commotion to die down before she leans in and says, "I'm sorry about before. It's not up to me how you and your sister get along."

Now I'm the one who takes her hand. I run my thumb over her knuckles. If we were alone, I'd kiss them—and more.

"It's okay. I was upset she didn't like my wardrobe choices. Not a big deal."

She studies me, and I watch her. Despite our dinner, she's still immaculate. Not a hair out of place, and her lipstick hasn't faded in the slightest. I, on the other hand, have marinara on my jumpsuit. It's only a small glob, and I did my best to wipe it off so you'd have to look for it to know it's there, but the fact remains I do know, and that plus Claire's comments before leave me feeling frumpy and disheveled.

Piper leans in so her lips are in line with my ear. Jono and his friends are laughing again, so anyone watching us will assume we're trying to hear each other over the noise.

"What I should have said before is you look hot as fuck," she says softly. "When we get back to the hotel, I'm going to show you exactly what I do with people I think are hot as fuck."

I freeze, and Piper sits back just far enough we can look at each other. The vision she describes makes me shiver, but on top of it comes a memory of a ten- or eleven-year-old Piper, deep in her space camp phase, ambushing me on the way home from school to ask me to sign her petition to rein- state Pluto as a planet. The juxtaposition is so absurd that I burst out laughing. For a second, Piper looks alarmed, but then she joins me, throwing her head back as we laugh. The whole room seems to be laughing, though the others can't know our joke.

"I'm sorry," Piper says, wiping her eyes. "That was really corny."

"No." I shake my head. "No, it was great. Great for my ego, anyway. Thank you."

Dinner wraps up with a couple of quick speeches. Lots of promises to Jono and Claire about how tomorrow will be the best day of their lives. Someone makes an alpaca joke that has Claire visibly flinching, but overall, everyone genuinely seems to be enjoying themselves.

Piper sits next to me in the rental as we drive back to the hotel. She's like a furnace radiating heat, and I only want to curl up in her. Except we've more or less come back to the hotel in a caravan, with Jono and Claire leading the way, and as I park the rental and get out, we're immediately swarmed by them and both halves of the wedding party, who ferry us inside for more drinks. I try to slip off, but Madison has her arm looped in mine and is holding on to me like a giggling boa constrictor. Piper's on her other side and glances over the top of Madison's head with a mournful expression, clearly as sad as I am to be diverted yet again. We'll get there, though. Even if I have to pull the hotel fire alarm and get everyone else out of the building, we're going to get there.

Drinks are poured. The atmosphere is much more low-key than the bachelorette the night before. Claire's sitting in Jono's lap, and the groomsmen flirt with willing brides-maids. A few try to slide up to me, but nothing kills a poten-tial suitor's aspirations faster than "Let me tell you about the proper ratios for embalming fluid." Most slink away quickly, looking for more receptive pastures.

One though—I think he said his name is Logan, but he's not one of Jono's med school friends, so I don't really know him—seems to take my chosen profession as a challenge.

"That's so cool," he says, eyes twinkling more with whisky than real enthusiasm. "So you, like, get to see what dead people look like on the inside? After they're dead, I mean? What's it like? Are they cold? Is it gross?"

The question is gross. A body is a body. There's nothing gruesome about internal organs, and the whole point of funeral services is to treat the people who come through with respect. It's not a freak show.

Piper appears at my side and even slips a protective arm around my waist. Or maybe she's getting ready to hold me back when I launch myself at this dickhead. But he's clearly still sober enough to realize—after a longish silence on my part—that he's said the wrong thing. His oblivious smile fades as Piper and I take simultaneous sips from our drinks —at least tonight we've skipped the penis straws—and watch as he, too, slides from his bar stool and rejoins the main conversation.

"The stereotype of the man-hating lesbian is terrible and reductionist," Piper says, "but woman are way better at conversation every single time."

"Among other things." I pout when she grins. "Can we please get out of here?"

But before she can answer, Claire bounds up to us, throwing her arms around my neck. Her cheeks are flushed, but her glass is still mostly full, and when she kisses my cheek, her hands are steady.

"Kate, are you having fun?" she asks.

"Sure," I say on reflex because I don't want to start another fight.

She pats my shoulder. Maybe she's drunker than I initially thought, because she says, "You look amazing in this. Where did you get it?"

"I thought it was too severe?"

She hangs her head. "I'm sorry about before. I'm not trying to be some kind of bridezilla. I was freaked out after the whole . . ." She waves her hand over her face. Whatever she did to her bangs before is losing its fight with time and gravity. The line of stitches is visible when she shakes her head.

I sigh, because I'm not a monster and I can't imagine how she must feel after the day she's had.

"It's okay," I say. "You and me, we've always had different styles." In comparison to my maybe-not-so-severe jumpsuit, Claire's worn a dress that looks like someone ripped up a vintage couch to make a costume for a community theater production of *Oklahoma*. It has big pink roses, with a high neck and puffed sleeves and a skirt that goes most of the way to the floor. It's not something I would ever take off the rack, but on Claire it looks soft and feminine.

"Well . . ." She glances over her shoulder and smiles at Jono. "Not different styles everywhere."

I wait for the anger. The hurt. It's a reflex at this point. But maybe I've had enough wine with dinner and enough to drink here that it's slow to respond. Maybe it's already gone to bed for the night.

I glance at Piper, who's watching me quietly, then ask, "Are you liking Denver?"

It's not exactly forgiveness. Part of me is still waiting for an apology. But it's an olive branch. I haven't asked Claire anything about her life since they moved out here. Honestly, we've hardly talked in years. And that might actually be my fault. I know Claire's tried to reach out. She's sent texts and commented on social media posts. There are unanswered calls on my phone and voicemails that I never returned because I told myself she'd call again if it was important.

The surprise on her face at my question stings a little, but she says, "Yeah, it's good. We both work a lot, so we're still getting to know the city. Mom and Dad bought us passes for the ski season at Winter Park as a wedding gift, so we're going to get to explore more whenever Jonathan can get away from the hospital."

And that's it. The most normal conversation I've had with my sister in three years. Maybe longer.

Like he's heard his name, Jono comes over and slides an arm over Claire's shoulder. She smiles up at him, and for a second, it's the four of us. Imagine what it might be if this is the future: Claire and Jono, me and Piper. But that's getting way ahead of myself. Piper and I aren't a couple. We're barely even friends. We're long-term acquaintances with a growing sexual attraction. Once we go home, I'm back to

Albany and she'll return to Vermont. It's not like we've ever kept in touch before.

The wedding pheromones must be invading my brain.

I get to my feet and make a big production of yawning before the feelings between me and Claire get any more awkward. Feels like we might be making progress. Let's not chance it by me staying here any longer.

"I'm going to bed," I say. "Big day tomorrow."

"No." Claire tugs on my hand. "Not yet." For once, I genuinely believe she wants me to stay, but I still think it's better to end this on a high note.

"I'm invoking my right as the older sister. I can't party like I used to." Honestly, as parties go, this one is pretty tame. The bar is empty except for our little group, and while everyone's having a good time, there's no sign that this will go beyond a few drinks.

They don't protest again as I head across the lobby. The space is quiet. Even the front desk is empty. I walk to the elevator and wait while the numbers tick down. A pair of black patent leather high heels click on the floor behind me. I smile as Piper comes to stand beside me, but we don't say anything until we're in the elevator and she punches the button for her floor.

"Are you trying to seduce me?" I ask as we start to rise.

She pushes up her glasses. "Is it working?"

I've never wanted anything more in my life.

9

"It's really unfair that you, a mere friend, get a room to yourself," I say, as we walk down the hall. "While I, honored older sister, have to sleep with Aunt Lois."

She laughs as she steps in front of me and puts her hands on my hips. The flounce of her skirt presses against my thighs.

"Are you really complaining that I'm not sharing a room right now?" Her mouth is so close to mine that I can see where the red is finally starting to wear away at the edges.

"No," I say petulantly. "Just that it's not fair. If anyone should be sleeping with Aunt Lois, it's you."

She rolls her eyes and pinches me, and I muffle a squeal as I jump forward, closing the last of the space between us. She catches me in a kiss, lips soft and inviting as I melt into her.

Piper. Little Piper.

I have to stop thinking about her like that. She's clearly not a child. She's a grown woman who knows what she wants, and somehow, she wants me, despite how perpetually messy I am.

"Still upset about the room?" she asks as we part. "Or should we make out in the hall more?"

I glance around, remembering that random family members might be lurking behind any one of these doors and I still don't want to be part of some awful bridal party cliche, even though nothing I feel when Piper touches me is awful.

"Lead the way. I'll behave."

I expect her to pounce on me the second we're through the door. Honestly, I'm ready to do the pouncing myself, but before I can, she's gone to the room's small mini fridge and is pulling out two small bottles of sparkling water. She twists the top off one with a fizzing hiss and hands me the second.

"Are you trying to sober me up?" I try for a charming smile, but I'm not sure it works. "Because honestly, I didn't have that much to drink tonight."

She studies me as she blows softly over the lip of her bottle. It makes a high whistling sound.

"I just want to make sure you're really sure. That you won't wake up and regret this in the morning." Her gaze drops away from me. "Like last time."

Oh, shit. I've apologized for that, right? I feel like I have. But if she needs me to do it again, I will. Even if I wasn't hoping for more with her tonight, I'd do it again, because she's Piper. She's been a friend and a sister to me for most of our lives, and if I ever made her feel like less, that's my fault.

Slowly, I take her bottle and set it down, along with mine. She won't quite meet my gaze, so I clasp her hands, kissing the back of them, then turning them over so I can kiss the sensitive skin at the base of each of her wrists.

"You were everything that night," I say as she shivers under my touch. "I was in such a bad place. I was hurt and looking for any way to lash out at Claire and Jono. I'm sorry that you got caught up in it. It was shitty and selfish. But I promise to look after you tonight and that I won't have any regrets in the morning. Honestly, you might be the best part of this whole weekend. I'm so glad you're here."

She smiles at that, lifting her perfect red lips to mine. She is so sweet, and I'm sorry. So sorry. Over and over. I try to tell her with my kisses, and slowly, her confidence returns. She grabs at my clothes in great handfuls, pulling us together until we're touching all the way down. Breasts, hands, hips, knees. She steps out of her heels but still stands on her toes, like she can't even bear to be that far away from me. I gather her up and there's so much of her. All the fabric and the sweet body beneath.

"Piper," I sigh. "Jesus, Piper, please."

Her nails drag over my back, making me arch, until the clasp at my neck comes loose and the front of the jumpsuit tumbles down to my waist. She mouths at my collarbones while she also reacquaints herself with my breasts and nipples. I push the feather-light fabric from my hips until I'm left wearing nothing but my shoes and the nude-colored seamless briefs that are my staple for pretty much all occasions.

Despite her impatience, Piper takes a step back to study me with an arched eyebrow, and I have to resist the urge to cover myself. Instead, I sink down on the bed, leaning back on my elbows so she can see anything she wants.

"What are the odds I can get you to agree that you'll only ever wear this when we're together?" she asks.

I bite my lip. The heat in her gaze makes me feel sexy. Powerful. There's a comfort, a safety in being with Piper. This is new for us, but we're not new to each other, and that goes such a long way.

"What about you? I was told there would be an exhibit of the finer points of corsetry if I behaved myself." Not that I intend to behave myself much longer. I slide a hand over my stomach and then lower, over the front of my underwear. Piper watches me, teeth caught between her lower lip. I linger, feeling the prickly curls of hair beneath my fingertips. I want so much more, but I want to see what's under that spectacular dress.

When I prompt her with an eyebrow, she lets go of her lip with a grin and lifts an arm to undo the zipper at the side of her dress. She pulls it off, one shoulder at a time, keeping her eyes on me the whole way, and it's like unwrapping the sexiest present I've ever seen. The lace slides from her skin, and slowly, the top of the corset becomes visible, pushing her breasts up and cinching her waist in tight.

"That can't be comfortable," I say.

"You get used to it." She pulls the dress down, rocking a bit from side to side to get the material to slide over her hips. There's a half inch of pale skin visible between the corset and her thong, and I scramble to the floor, rushing inelegantly over the carpet until I'm kneeling in front of her, hands on her hips.

"Stay like that," I say. She's watching me with hooded eyes, and her lips are parted. I press a kiss to that line of bare flesh and Piper freezes, holding her breath. I kiss again, from hip bone to hip bone, pressing my thumbs against the soft skin. Honestly, with the way her breath starts again, coming out in short staccato puffs, I might be able to do this all night, but as I reach the center of her lower belly again, I stare up at her, dragging a single finger over the front of the thong until soft wetness beneath that tiny scrap of fabric begins to soak through.

"Kate." Piper puts a hand on my shoulder to steady herself.

"Come here." I stand, bringing her with me. She probably expects we're headed to the bed, so instead I lean against the simple hotel room dresser. It might actually be real wood instead of the usual cheap particleboard, because when I settle back, it doesn't so much as creak. I spin Piper around, examining the back of the corset. The tip of the swan tattoo's wing peeks over the top, while a trail of laces fall over the small of her back. I pull at the bow, but it's tied snug in a complicated knot.

"Hmm," I say, as my sexy fantasies vanish. I will not be thwarted by something as simple as a piece of string, and yet, as I pull at it, the whole thing only seems to get tighter.

"Wait," Piper says. She puts her hands on her waist and exhales slowly. The whole corset squeezes in more, followed by a popping sound, then her rib cage expands on her long inhale as the corset comes loose.

"Stop," I say, wrapping my arms around her, feeling the gap where she's opened the corset from the front. "That's cheating."

"It's expedient," she says, trying to wriggle free of my grasp on a laugh. I release her just enough that she can let the corset drop to the ground between us. It's surprisingly heavy, and something about the thought of her sitting there all night, pressed inside of it, having to measure her breaths and stay perfectly upright, is such a turn-on for me. Maybe it's because half the time when I'm with my family, I feel like I can barely breathe. Maybe she understands a little too.

She backs herself into me, settling her bottom between my thighs. We're the same now. A few scraps of fabric are all that's left between us. She turns her head over her shoulder, tipping her chin up to ask for my kiss, and I'm so very happy to give it to her. I roam with my hands, feeling the creamy skin beneath. She's got a mole to the left side of her belly button, and her breasts are heavy weights in my palms. I flick the nipples a few times, but it doesn't seem to do as much for her as it does for me, so I resume my explorations, finding the spots where she's ticklish along her sides and learning the way she whimpers when I take her earlobe in my teeth and tug.

Touching her is familiar and exciting at the same time. Because it's Piper. How could it not be familiar? And yet it's not, because at no point when we were growing up did it ever cross my mind that we might be like this someday. Or that *I* might be like this. It took me way too long to reconsider my sexuality.

"Kate," Piper says breathlessly, "stop thinking and touch me."

"Pretty sure I *was* touching you," I say, nosing at her ear. We both know I'm misunderstanding to be cute, and she grabs my hand where I'm currently running my fingers over the front of her thong and slips it under the waistband. Easy enough to guess what she wants. I'm fully sitting on the dresser now, legs spread with Piper cradled between them. I pull back my hand long enough to help her slip the thong off, then go back where she wants me, dipping a fingertip between the slick folds to the velvety-soft flesh between them.

"Yes." She sighs, pushing her hips up. Kissing at this angle is awkward, but we do our best while I stroke back and forth for a moment, feeling her needy wetness before I find the small bud of her clit at the top. I circle around it, and she trembles.

"Like that?" I ask. She nods jerkily, tipping her head back so her throat is exposed. I drag my teeth along it as I keep working her clit, finding the little movements that make her twitch. Sometimes she takes my wrist, showing me what she likes or holding me still while she rubs against me on her own. I take it all in, getting to know her. Getting to know us. Like this.

"Can you come this way?" I ask. Even if she can't, I might be able to just from the little breathy moans she makes as I circle her flesh with my thumb. The junction of my thighs is slick, and I ache with the need to be touched.

She presses her lips together as she shakes her head. "Doesn't mean you should stop though. God, Kate. I've wanted you so bad all day. This is so good."

I appreciate her enthusiasm, but I can do more. I know I can.

"Come to bed," I say. She steps away from me with a pout but makes her way to the bed as instructed while I pull off my underwear. Since she's alone, she's been given a big king-size instead of the two doubles in my room with Lois, and the extra space feels excessive, even once we're both on the mattress, because we can't do anything but get as close as possible.

We face each other, kissing, and Piper puts a hand to the small of my back, pushing me forward until she can press a knee between my thighs. There's no way to hide how wet I am, but she smiles against my lips.

"Oh, you poor baby. I was being selfish."

"Not at all. You were—" But whatever I was going to say gets cut off when she rolls me to my back and strokes a confident index finger over my clit. I nearly come off the bed at the contact, and I start begging before I can help myself. "Please. Please. Piper."

"It's okay," she says, voice soft and husky. "I've got you."

She kisses me while she plays with my clit. I practically shove myself at her. She's hardly started and already, my orgasm is so close. Between the pressure of her fingers and the wet intrusion of her tongue between my lips, everything is a slick invasion that has me going to hot liquid.

"Piper—" The orgasm hits me so fast, I practically scream into her mouth. She keeps going, teasing my throbbing clit as I shake and spasm. I've got my face buried in her neck, and the sounds coming out of my throat are high, short bursts of nothing but pleasure.

"Shh." Piper pets my hair like I'm a restless child, and I wait for the twitching to stop.

"You're amazing," I say.

"More like motivated." She makes a purring sound against my lips. "Been waiting to hear that for more than a year. When you come, it's like you're singing. It's beautiful. You're beautiful."

We're too close for her to really be able to see me blush, but I bury my face in the pillow anyway. She strokes my back and kisses my shoulder, and it's only a moment before I turn back to her.

"What can I do?" I ask.

She bumps her nose against mine. "If I'd known this was going to happen, I'd have brought some toys. I bought this fingertip vibe a month ago that would make your toes curl."

"Pretty sure you did that on your own. What else?" I slip a hand between her thighs. She said it wouldn't be enough, but that doesn't mean I can't keep the mood going.

"Depends on what you're comfortable with," she says, voice matter-of-fact, and I appreciate it. Things are going well, but honestly, I'm out of my depth. We didn't get this far last time, and it's not like I've done much research since.

"Whatever you want," I say.

"You're cute." She rolls, bringing me with her, and spreads her legs, so I settle between them. "Fingers. More fingers, actually. Or your tongue, if you're up for it."

"It's cunnilingus, not BASE jumping."

"Not everyone likes to. Especially straight girls."

"I think we're proving definitively that I'm not very straight."

She stills. The room isn't fully dark, and her eyes turn serious as she looks up at me. "It would be okay if you thought you were. For this. For right now. I've wanted you pretty much since I was fifteen, but if you only want to play around, that's okay. I'm not expecting anything after this weekend."

I fight back a defiant prickle. She shouldn't feel like she has to give me an out or let me off the hook. Is this still about last time? It sucks that I've left this question mark between us, but the only way I can think to answer it is to see tonight through to the end. And maybe longer. She said she has no expectations once we're back east, but would it be so bad? So hard? Albany to Vermont isn't that far, is it?

Slowly, I creep down her body, kissing a trail between her breasts and over her belly button.

"Let me know if I do something wrong," I say. Before I can reach my destination, a pillow thumps gently over the back of my head.

"That will help," she says and lifts up her hips, so I slide the pillow beneath.

Her pubic hair is soft but trimmed short. I spread her gently open, and I barely have time to put the tip of my tongue to her clit before she jumps.

"What?" I ask.

"Sorry." She settles down again. "Just excited."

"Hush." I nip at the inside of her thigh, and she squeaks. "You'll give me performance anxiety."

Am I amazing? Doubtful. Jono was never much for oral sex unless he was on the receiving end, so I only have so much to refer back to. For Claire's sake, I hope he's expanded his horizons. But now's not really the time to be mulling over my sister's sex life, because as I grow my own skillset, Piper squeals above me.

"Oh God. Yes. Just like that."

I take a quick second to glance up. Her hands are moving restlessly over her body, and her head rolls from side to side. I take her clit between my lips, sucking gently, and she groans.

"That's good too," she says, like I'm presenting color options to paint a living room. But when I suck again, increasing the pressure, her breath gets strangled. I alternate, sucking and licking, and she fists the sheets as she pushes her hips up against my mouth. I wrap my arms over the backs of her thighs, holding her in place as I work, finding the rhythm that makes her breathing come faster.

"Kate. Katie. Oh, I'm—" But I don't need the warning. The way her muscles twitch and spasm under me is notice enough. I keep going even as she thrashes, holding her close, pressing my fingers so tightly against her hip bones that I should probably worry about bruising, but I don't think either of us will complain.

Finally, she goes slack in my hands, and her breathing slows. She makes a happy sound as I crawl back up against her side. She rolls to squeeze me tight.

"You're a fast learner," she says. She kisses me, and I should feel self-conscious about the fact that I had my chin buried in her pussy seconds ago, but she doesn't seem to care, so I let the worry slip away.

"I'll do better next time," I say, wanting her to know how much I want there to be a next time. I'm not ashamed or confused. There will be no regrets later. I'm simply . . . happy. At ease for the first time in what feels like forever. Lying here with Piper is the most relaxed I've felt in ages, and it's not just the orgasms.

She slips a hand between my thighs, and even though I'm not usually one for multiple orgasms, the way my body lights up as she dips a finger inside me says tonight might be an exception.

"Trust me," she says as my skin goes hot. "You're doing just fine."

10

The concept of a walk of shame is deeply rooted in misogyny. There's nothing shameful about walking down the hall after the best night of sex of my life. Or at least, that's what I tell myself as I try not to jump at every sound that might be a door opening or someone just around the corner. Because as much as I have no regrets about what happened last night, there's no doubt that if the wrong person—my mom, Claire, Grandma—finds me still in last night's clothes on a floor of the hotel where I have no obvious business being, I'll be accused of causing a scene or a distraction on the day of the wedding. I don't want what happened between me and Piper to be diminished by having to do damage control with my family.

Still, there's no avoiding Aunt Lois as I let myself back into our room. She's sitting in the armchair by the window sipping some coffee, and she peers over a pair of wire-framed glasses at me with a knowing grin.

"You put your shirt on backwards."

On reflex my hand goes to my throat, looking for a tag, before I remember I'm not wearing a shirt. I give her a sour look.

"Very funny."

"Did you get lost?"

"You're up early," I say.

"Did you and Piper finally seal the deal?"

"What?"

Lois cackles as she sets her mug down. "You two were making eyes at each other all evening. Not hard to guess what happened next."

I grimace. We so weren't making eyes. Were we? And if we were, did anyone else notice?

Lois comes across the room and folds me into a tight hug. "I'm so proud of you. Baby's first bisexual panic."

My ribs creak before she lets me go. "Thanks."

"Or maybe not the first," she says with a waggle of her eyebrows. "All those months alone. Women in foreign places that aren't so uptight about these things. Maybe you've been holding out on me. You know, there was this time I went to Iceland, and—"

"Stop. Stop, Aunt Lois, I don't want to know about—" But it's me that stops, because the next words out of my mouth would have been *wild sapphic adventures*, and while that is true, there's a different truth beneath it that freezes me in my tracks. "Aunt Lois, are you . . ." I'm not sure what word I want to use to finish that sentence, but fortunately, I don't have to choose.

"Well, of course, dear. Isn't the whole point of being the unattached, childless sister to dally with whoever strikes my fancy?" She laughs like she isn't sharing completely new information with me.

"Pretty sure no one says *dally* these days." I shove my hands in the jumpsuit pockets and hunch my shoulders.

She pats my cheek, furthering the illusion that I'm a petulant six-year-old. "Not the point, dear. You spent so much time being one kind of person."

"A straight kind of person?" I can't hide the bitterness in my voice.

"It's not about straight or queer. You were on track to be a doctor from the time you got a plastic doctor's kit at Christmas the year you were in kindergarten. I could see it in your eyes."

"Because I loved it."

"Because you were good at it. School. Science. Studying. You stayed with Jonathan because he fit into that straight line too. That's not the same thing as love."

Out of nowhere, I want to cry. I haven't cried about any of this in years. There were a few weepy nights at a hostel in Paris, but after I figured out my trip and changed directions, I was fine. And maybe that's the point. I started out with the kind of destinations Jono and I had always planned on visiting once we weren't consumed with med school, and it turned out there wasn't much there for me. Maybe this is what Lois is trying to get me to acknowledge on a bigger scale.

Still, stubbornness is a family trait. I shake my head. "You can't possibly know this. We saw you a few times a year while I was growing up. How do you know about who I was at school?"

She puts an arm around my shoulder. "Older sisters have to stick together, regardless of generation. I know what it's like to have all those expectations put on you. And I'm so proud of you for doing it your way, anyway."

I'm annoyed, though I do my best to smile. Not so much annoyed at Lois in general, but more that what she's saying makes sense, and I feel ridiculous for not having thought about it this way before. Distantly, the annoyance spreads to Jono, who dumped me and tore up my life's road map in the process. The jerk. He deserves no credit for any of this, and yet if he hadn't, we'd have been married by now, and I'd be stressing my way through a residency, and I wouldn't have spent last night in Piper's arms.

I cough to clear my throat. "I need a shower. We're meeting at the salon in thirty minutes, and I'm starving too."

"I'll make you a coffee," Lois says. "And see if the hotel does room service."

———

THE SALON IS IN TOWN, and we go in two cars. Piper and I sit squished next to each other in the backseat of Jono's green convertible, and even though the heat of her body warms one side of mine, it's nearly painful not to be able to touch her the way I want to. The way her hand twitches toward me from time to time says she feels the same way.

Claire's organized for our hair and makeup to be done, but there's been some kind of mix-up as to how many stylists were supposed to be there, and Claire's not happy, though I can't tell if it's more or fewer people than the five black-clad women who are eyeing us while the scent of hairspray lingers in the air. A photographer has also shown up, and she circles around us with a camera that looks like it might be capable of signaling extraterrestrial life forms while documenting our big day.

"Kate can have her hair done last," Claire says. "Not like there's much to do, anyway."

She's not wrong, but the way she says it makes it sound like my hair is just one more disappointment she has to contend with on this overwhelming weekend. There had been an email chain that went around several months ago about hairstyles and whether it was better for the bridal party to match their style to the bride or counter it by going for updos if she wore hers down and vice versa. I pretty much stayed out of it because any response would have inevitably been met with demands phrased as "I'm just asking" about whether or not I planned to grow my hair out when I definitely did not. Besides, with how short most of it is, the best growing it out would have achieved is to make me look like an overwhelmed hedgehog.

It's a flurry of activity now, though, for the others. Wash, blow dry, hot rollers, enough bobby pins that you could build an impressive art installation. There is much squealing when the box with Claire's veil is produced, and more when she pulls out a separate bunch of gift boxes that all contain pink and white floral hair combs that we're supposed to incorporate into our finished look.

"You okay?" Piper sits beside me in one of the chairs for waiting victims—I mean, customers.

I smile at her. "Never better. A little tired." It was not my most restful night, though I have no regrets. I watched the sunrise with Piper's face between my thighs and oh, boy was that an out-of-body experience. Hopefully I didn't wake the neighbors, but there wasn't much to be done to muffle the waves of pleasure that poured over me as she drew out my orgasm with the tip of her tongue.

Her face scrunches in amusement at my weary expression. "I know what you mean. Might need a nap later."

I smother a groan. Finding an hour or two to be together, even to sleep close to her, sounds like heaven. But there's no chance. We're on Claire's clock from now until the last speech is spoken. Speaking of . . .

"How's your speech coming?" Piper asks.

"I think I've got it worked out." I've been making notes on my phone while I sit here. Honestly, I'm not convinced what I've really come up with is any better than "love is patient, love is kind," but I hope Claire and Jono hear the truth in it. They found each other, and they're committed enough that Claire's moved all the way across the country knowing Jono will work all the time and she'll have to make a life for herself away from everyone she knows. If it were a fling, she'd have given up ages ago. That last part isn't in my speech, though. Bottom line, I hope they're happy. The distance—both in terms of time and geography—means I have room to work on my feelings without getting myself into trouble.

"Are you flying back to New York tomorrow?" I ask. Maybe we can sit together if we're on the same flight.

But she shakes her head sadly. "I've got a flight to Burlington with a stop in Detroit."

Poor planning on our part. Though no one could have seen this coming. Hoped, maybe, but not enough to organize a travel itinerary.

"Are you coming back home over the summer?" I hadn't planned on going down to Mom and Dad's much over the next few months when I'd spent so much time with them here, but if Piper will be back in town, I could be convinced.

Her grin turns crooked, but before she can answer, my name is called, and I find myself in the stylist's chair.

"So," she says, running her fingers over my scalp. The disappointment in her gaze is obvious. "Guess we're not putting your hair up like the others?"

The floral clip is in my hands. The flowers are made of silk, and small pink beads glint up at me in the light. I hold it up to the stylist.

"Put this wherever you think is best."

She does a passable job, I guess? Or she does what's possible, which basically means slicking my hair back and pinning the comb into place behind my ear on the few strands that are long enough. She uses a mountain of product and makes me shake my head repeatedly to ensure it's not going to fall out, but it holds, and I'm sent on to makeup. The others are all done except for Piper, who sits in the chair next to me. The desired makeup look is very simple and natural. I mourn the loss of Piper's stunning red lips. The photographer takes a series of pictures of me while the makeup artist applies lipstick, and I hope I look thoughtful rather than like a gasping fish.

Finally, we're done. My face feels heavy in the way it always does when I bother putting on a full coat of makeup, but the effect in the mirror is pretty. Even the flowers don't look too silly once you take in the whole package.

However, the coffee Lois made me has now settled in my bladder and needs my attention. I excuse myself to the bathroom while Claire and the others sort out payment.

When I come back, the salon is empty except for Claire and Piper, who are standing by the door.

"No, really," Claire says. "I appreciate it."

"It was no problem." Piper laughs. Her face looks so different in her bridesmaid makeup, but her laughter makes me smile. "I've always liked Kate."

I freeze. I'm at the end of the hall that leads back to the bathroom, and I press against the wall.

Claire sighs. "I was so worried she was going to do something this weekend."

"She's fine. We're all adults, Claire."

"Still, I really appreciate you keeping an eye on her. I know babysitting wasn't on the official list of bridesmaids duties, but she's been so angry this year, and I was worried—"

"It's not even babysitting." The relaxed sound of Piper's voice makes my throat go tight. I squeeze my eyes tight, locking in the tears that threaten for the second time this morning. "I've had a lot of fun."

Fun. Like it's all been a game. Of course it has. They've probably been planning this for a while. Maybe even since last year after the engagement party.

"Where is she?" Claire asks, and she must be talking about me.

"We've still got time," Piper says.

"Yeah, but I'm hungry. I was so nervous this morning that I skipped breakfast. There's a bakery across the street. I'm going to go get a muffin or something. Meet us over there?" Then, the sound of a bell chiming signals that the salon door opens and closes, and the space falls into silence.

I stay just as quiet, though how Piper doesn't hear my heart racing, I don't know. I'm so angry that I'm shaking. Babysitting? Like Piper had been some minder to trail after me and make sure I didn't cause a scene? Is that what this has all been? Suddenly, my sunrise orgasms don't feel so special.

"Kate?" Piper calls, and her heels clack on the floor like she's walking toward me. "You okay back there?"

I have a few choices.

One: find a back door and make a run for it.

Two: tell Piper I heard everything and deal with this as adults.

Or three: cause the scene they're all expecting and spoil Claire's big day.

"Yeah, what's up?" I come around the corner, and my smile feels so forced that it's a miracle my face doesn't crack in half.

Piper's smile, on the other hand, is blindingly bright as she pulls me close and kisses me.

"Someone might see," I say, trying to extricate myself.

"They're all across the street."

"You'll smudge the makeup."

She laughs against my lips. "Doesn't matter if we're both wearing the same color, and anyway, Madison has a tube for touch-ups."

"You've thought of everything," I say, though I don't know how the words get around the lump in my throat.

She takes my hand and I let her lead me to the door, just like she's been leading me around all weekend.

Four: pretend like everything is fine for the sake of my family and wait for the weekend to be over so I never have to talk to Piper again.

11

SOMEONE—AUNT LOIS, I GUESS—HAS TAKEN MY BRIDESMAID dress to Claire's room while we were at the salon. Whoever did it, they're on my rapidly growing shit list, because the walk from the lobby to my room and up to Claire's was the time I was going to use to clear my head, and instead, I'm thrust directly into the thick of it. The dresses are all laid out in the closet, with the photographer clicking away like she's discovered the next big fashion trend. A bottle of champagne is chilling in a bucket, and Claire and the others squeal as Piper pops the cork and starts pouring into flutes. I try to decline when she hands me one, because keeping a clear head is going to be so important for the next few hours, but Claire announces it's time for a toast, and the camera is already clicking again before I've fully grasped the glass.

Every snap of the shutter makes me blink. Every crack of laughter from the bridesmaids makes my head ache. The brush of Piper's fingers on my back as she does up the zipper of my dress makes me flinch.

"Sorry," she says softly. "Did I pinch you?"

"I'm fine." Though already, I'm sweating inside the chiffon, and the lace on my chest itches terribly.

"Hey." She tugs at my elbow. "Are you okay? You're quiet."

Because I'm trying not to scream? Because all I want to ask her is what was true and what was a lie? Because my whole family thinks I need to be treated like a bomb about to go off and now all I want to do *is* go off, because why am I the problem here?

Before I can say—for the millionth time— that I'm fine, the door opens, and Mom comes in. She is everything the mother of the bride should be when she's already prone to overreacting. There are tears when she sees Claire in her dress, then more tears from Claire because Mom is crying, then even further weeping when they both realize their makeup is running and we have to start all over again. Piper hovers at my elbow the whole time despite my efforts to create space, and it's only when the photographer says, "Okay, now some shots with Mom and her two daughters," that I finally escape, except now I'm stuck standing in a happy cluster with Mom and Claire and we have to pretend we're laughing at a joke that no one's said, and I can't help but feel it's me. I'm the joke.

I scratch at my chest where the material itches my skin, and I snag a nail on the lace. It pulls a thread free, and the polish is chipped. I ball my hand into a fist and hide it behind my back. At some point, someone hands me a bouquet—cream and pink roses that Claire is upset about because apparently, they're the wrong pink—and we make our way down to the lobby where Jono and his groomsman and family are waiting. There are more pictures: Jono getting teary as Claire walks toward him like a shimmering goddess, shots with the bride and groom and each family member individually. Whenever I'm not required to pose, somehow Piper is always standing at my side, but she doesn't say anything in public, and I don't speak either, pretending instead to be thoroughly engrossed in the supposed nuptial magic around us.

Jono and Claire are getting married at the summit of Everwood Peak. They've opened the chairlift especially for us. The bridal party and immediate family go up early before the rest of the guests. I try to give Piper the slip and ride up with Mom and Dad, but the fates conspire against us this one last time, because my parents wind up having to help Grandma, and I'm left at the end of the line.

Piper gives me a nervous smile as I look around for a way to escape.

"Guess it's just us," she says.

I'm trying so hard. Really, I am. My insides are a bonfire of hurt feelings, but I'm doing my very best to hide it all under a metaphorical bushel or whatever.

"Guess it is."

It's the worst. Worse than being in a car, because there at least I'd have the excuse of needing to focus on the road. Worse than last night at the rehearsal dinner when all I wanted to do was touch her and find out what it was like to have her alone, because now I know what that's like and I'm afraid it was all a lie.

"You're quiet," Piper says. Everything is quiet. Really couldn't be any quieter. We're more than thirty feet in the air on a mountain that's closed for the season. The loudest sounds are a bird in one of the trees and the rattle of the wheels as the chair passes over each of the towers.

"Not much to say." I study my flowers. The edges of the cream roses are already turning brown.

"Is this about Jono? Or Claire? Did she say something to you?"

Fury at her kind tone burns under my scalp. I squeeze my bouquet so hard that the nubs of thorns that were cut off press into my palms.

"No," I say. "But she said something to you. I heard you talking at the salon."

"You heard us . . ." she says, but I see the moment she goes pale. "Oh God, Kate."

"I'm not a problem that needs to be managed, Piper."

"No, I know. Kate, I—" She reaches for me, then seems to reconsider. "It's not like that."

"Like what? Like you've been following me around like a nanny waiting for me to dump juice on my shirt and pitch a fit that it's wet?"

"Claire asked me . . . She said . . ." Piper drops her head, and my heart starts to break off into little pieces. "It hasn't been easy for her, you know. She knows you're upset, but you never talk about it."

"And instead of coming to me herself and asking if I was okay with her marrying my ex, she sent you to spy on me instead?" I have to look off into the distance to blink back hot tears. The day is perfect. Exactly what you'd hope for if you were planning a mountaintop wedding. I hate it.

"She's my friend, Kate," Piper says, sounding sad, and I bite back the immediate question about what that makes me. A pet project, maybe. A quick lay.

"You know what? It's fine. It doesn't matter. We're almost done all of this, and then you can tell Claire I hope she and Jono are very happy."

"No." This time, Piper does reach for me. She rests her hand on mine where I've left it on the chair safety bar. "It doesn't have to be like that. She cares about you. I care about you."

"You care enough that you'd seduce me to shut me up?"

The accusation is meaner and uglier than I intend it to

be, and when I glance at Piper, the color is back in her cheeks. She lets go of my hand.

"It wouldn't hurt you, you know," she says, and her voice has gone flat. "To admit this could be a nice time."

I snort. "Sure."

"A wedding is supposed to be fun. You could be having fun, Kate, if you let yourself. Instead, you're sulking and doing your best to prove you're not like the other girls. It's not a good look. Being older doesn't mean anything anymore. We're not kids."

"Yeah, I figured that out last night when you had your tongue on my clit, thank you very much."

That's it. That's the nail in the coffin, and I know a thing or two about coffins. Piper jerks her head back as if I've slapped her, and regret twists through me like a muscle spasm. I hold in the rest of my angry words because they'll only confirm what she's accused me of, and I can't give her that satisfaction.

We finish the rest of the ride in silence, and it's even more all-consuming than before. I can barely look at her, because every time she inhales a little too loudly, I worry she might be crying, and I don't think I could handle the knowledge I made Piper cry.

She's wrong, of course. Not having fun is not a choice. This whole weekend has been chaos from the moment I put that green penis straw in my mouth. My family is ridiculous and so caught up in their own problems that no one has looked in on me once. No one except maybe Aunt Lois, but she would be as pissed as I am to find out that sleeping with Piper was about keeping me out of the way. So much for epic bisexual adventures. The whole thing was a manipulation from the beginning.

Everyone is waiting as we step off the chair, and once

again we're swept up into the commotion of a wedding day. More pictures, posed against the dramatic backdrop of the Rockies. I try to stand at the end of the line of bridesmaids while Piper stands closer to Claire, but the photographer doesn't like that and wants us arranged by height, so of course I spend too many uncomfortable minutes standing so close to her that her elbow occasionally grazes my arm or chest. More than once, I'm told to smile—both by the photographer and by my mom—and I arrange my face into somewhere between a grin and a grimace and hope the photographer can fix it in post or whatever it is wedding photographers do.

The whole time, Claire and Jono are in a bubble of happy, pre-wedded bliss. They gaze up at each other and laugh and walk shoulder to shoulder from one location to the next, completely oblivious to anything and everything around them. The other bridesmaids flock after them, chattering happily as their dresses stream behind them in a cascade of fluttering pink chiffon, and I allow myself a single moment of self-recrimination over Piper's accusations —would it be so bad to be like them when they seem so happy?—before I go back to stewing instead.

Finally, the wedding starts. A flat space of land between the top of the lift and the summit lodge has been cleared for us, with rows of chairs set up for guests and an arched bower of limbs and more pink and cream roses erected to designate the place where Claire and Jono will say their vows. I walk up the aisle on legs that feel wooden and feet like lead weights. At the front, Jono is standing there. Once, he would have been waiting for me, but now he barely even glances at me before he's looking over my shoulder, waiting for Claire.

Does he know about Claire and Piper's arrangement?

Was he in on it? The conspiracy theories mount in my head. As I take my place at the front, I turn back to look at the guests assembled. Mom's crying, and Dad has an arm around her shoulders. Did they know too? Did Mom tell Claire she had to do something because I couldn't be trusted?

Across the aisle, Adrian and Ted watch their son proudly. Behind my parents, Aunt Lois watches me, and I try to give her a reassuring smile, but beyond her shoulder I catch a glimpse of Piper coming up the aisle, and my smile falters. Instead, I stare over all their heads, looking at the mountains around us and the town farther down the valley. It's pretty here. I wonder if they need a funeral director. But of course, that defeats my goal of being several time zones away from Claire and Jono's happy ending.

He says, "I do." So does she. Everyone claps as they kiss. Why can't I be happy for them? What part of me refuses to let go? They walk back down the aisle, and I follow on Logan's arm. His name is the only thing I know about him. I'm suddenly compelled to ask him everything. Where did he meet Jono? Does he live in Colorado too? What does he do for a living? Has he ever been backpacking around Australia? But it's too late. We reach the end of the procession, and he lets go of me to high-five his friends and get a jump on the bar before the rest of the guests descend.

Too late.

Small talk is the same as it has been all weekend: painful. Except now, Piper doesn't appear from time to time to ask me if I'm okay or if I want to sneak off to make out somewhere. The very memory of it leaves a bad taste in my mouth that I chase down with white wine. The fact that she doesn't come back to plead her case is another indication that she knows she fucked up. I wonder if she's told Claire that I found out about their plans, but of course, probably not. She's too considerate for that. No doubt she's doing like me: riding out these last few hours and hoping it all goes smoothly.

Dinner is served in a restaurant inside the lodge. Jono and Claire are given their own cozy table for two, and the whole bridal party is scattered among the rest of the guests instead of grouping us together. I'm seated at a table with Aunt Lois and Grandma.

"You doing okay?" Lois asks as I sit down, and I nod wordlessly while reaching for the wine bottle that is already open on the table and pour myself a glass. She watches me with a worried expression, so I do the polite thing and pour her one too.

The meal feels too loud and endless, but finally, one of the groomsmen gets up with a microphone in his hand and tells a story about meeting Jono on their first day of rotations at the hospital and how Jono was the kind of person you knew you could trust with your life. Madison gets up and talks about how Claire told her after the first date with Jono that she was going to marry him. I wonder when that might have been, then wonder if it really might be my fault I don't know. I never asked. I never asked Claire anything.

I pick at the last of my dinner and finish the glass of wine in front of me.

"And now, we're going to hear a few words from the bride's sister, Kate."

I cough on my wine. Oh, shit.

Love is patient, love is kind. I mutter it to myself over and over as I rise unsteadily and make my way to where Madison is holding out the microphone.

Love does not envy or boast.

Claire is watching me with nervous eyes as I take the mic, a silent plea for me not to say anything I shouldn't.

She could have asked.

My voice shakes as I raise the mic to my lips. "For those of you who don't know me, my name is Kate, and Claire is my baby sister."

12

I can't exactly say I have a captive audience. Even with all the guests sitting, servers move through the crowd as they collect dinner plates and deliver desserts, and people talk quietly among each other. They aren't expecting me to say anything profound.

Love is not arrogant or rude.

"I recognize that as the older sister, it's expected that I have some important life advice to share. But I think we can all agree, when it comes to what it takes for a long and happy marriage, I'm not exactly the most qualified person in the room."

A few appreciative chuckles ripple toward me. Probably safe to assume that everyone here knows—or has at least heard—I'm the groom's jilted ex. Let them laugh. The situation is unusual. I even catch Jono glancing nervously at Claire, but she's still watching me and doesn't see it.

"I haven't been the luckiest in love." Without meaning to, I scan the crowd until I find Piper's face. I nearly miss it, already so used to looking for her curvy silhouette and red lips instead of the muted costume she's put on for my sister. We're all pretending to be someone this weekend. "But honestly, I don't think love has much to do with luck. Someday, you look at the people around you and decide that one of them will be the right person for you."

The chuckles die. Everyone wants to hear about the fairy tale. How one day Jono woke up and found Claire standing beside him like a princess waiting for her prince and that was the end of that. But if they wanted the fairy tale, they should have asked someone else to talk.

"The important parts to making any relationship work are the same, regardless of whether you're married or dating, or even if you're friends." Again, I find Piper. She's staring down at the table. "Trust. Honesty. Treating each other like real people who are capable of making their own decisions."

A cough comes from the left side of the room, and when I look, my mom is glaring daggers at me. Don't make a scene, Katie. Don't spoil your sister's big day.

"Don't make assumptions about how people will behave. Even people you know better than anyone in the world. Everyone is going through something, and it doesn't hurt to ask how they're doing from time to time. Maybe the fight isn't even about whose turn it is to clean the bathroom or take out the garbage. If you'd just listen to each other instead of treating them like a child, you would . . ."

The room is dead silent now. No doubt they were expecting an anecdote about how when we were kids, Claire would make me play make-believe wedding games where she always insisted on being the bride. But I've spent the last few years being so angry with Jono and with her that I can't bring any of those to mind. Those happy memories of my little sister have vanished.

For the first time this weekend, a tear finally slides down my cheek. I slap a palm over it before it smears my makeup. I sniff and clear my throat. Chairs scrape on the floor as people shift, waiting for the mood to go back to celebration, but that's not the speech I can give. To do that would require me to be happy to be here, and I haven't let myself be happy. Not this weekend. Maybe not in a long time.

Another tear threatens to slip, and I squeeze my eyes shut, trying to compose myself. But instead of stern internal words telling me to cut it short and sit down again, all I can hear is Piper's accusation that I've done this to myself. That I've let the anger rule when I always had the choice to enjoy myself instead. Maybe not even forgive the past, but choose to celebrate Claire and Jono's happiness today.

I let out a deep exhale and open my eyes. Claire looks positively ill, and Jono is holding his breath. They're clinging to each other's hands, and that's the truth of it right there. They chose each other. I removed myself from the equation. Literally fled the country. I can't be mad they chose each other. I can only hope they continue to choose each other every day from now on. If they make it over the ultimate finish line together someday, then there can't be any second-guessing. No what-ifs. They were always meant to be.

"Don't go to bed angry," I say, and a few nervous giggles sound up from the crowd. "No, seriously. It's the worst cliche. You can get it stitched on a pillow if that's what it takes to remember it. But don't go to bed angry, and if you do, make sure you talk about it in the morning. It's too easy to let anger win, and once it does, it takes and takes. We're all human and we all make mistakes and get hurt sometimes, but don't let it win. There are so many good days coming." My voice strangles to nothing on the last word. This is so embarrassing. I'm struggling to hold myself together, but maybe this is the apology I've been waiting for all along. The apology to myself. Permission to let the anger go.

"Of course, makeup sex is pretty good too," I say, trying to smile. People laugh again as we sail back into familiar territory. I wrap up with general platitudes about how happy they look and how pretty Claire is and how if Jono ever hurts her, I'll put all my new mortuary know-how into making his death look like an accident. More laughs, and I walk back to my seat with rubbery legs and flaming cheeks. No one will quite meet my gaze when I sit down again, but Aunt Lois squeezes my hand.

"Good job, kiddo," she says, and I choke on a watery laugh, because I just made a whole speech at my sister's wedding about how I don't want to be treated like a child, yet somehow her words give me more comfort than anything has except lying curled up around Piper.

Piper. I glance toward her table, but she's not in her seat. Maybe she's gone to the bathroom. Before I can investigate, though, the lights in the room go down, and a spotlight on the dance floor comes on, where Jono and his groomsmen are positioned in some classic boy band stance. The music plays a familiar riff, and they launch into a ridiculous dance number that has the whole room cheering, especially when Jono slides across the floor on his knees, coming to a perfect stop at Claire's feet where she's seated, laughing and clapping. His face is bright as she pulls him up for a kiss that has everyone hooting.

They look so damn happy. So does everyone around me. They clap and sway in their chairs, clearly excited to really get the party started. They've chosen to be happy this weekend, even though back at home they've all got problems waiting for them. Bills to pay, bosses they hate. And sure, unless that shitty boss is here this weekend, they don't have quite the immediate and direct reminder in front of them that I do, but they've still chosen to set all that aside to have a good time here.

Logan is hovering at my elbow as Claire and Jono take their formal first dance. As the music changes, he says, "Wanna dance?"

I eye him. He's nice enough to look at. Good old boy features and the beginnings of a dad bod on his late-twenties frame. If he's hoping this is the beginning of a drunken wedding night hookup, he'll be deeply disappointed.

"Do you have a girlfriend, Logan?" I ask, and if he's surprised, he covers it well on a laugh while he holds up his left hand to show me the gold band around his fourth finger.

"My wife's at home with our six-month-old twins. Do you want to see a picture?"

So we don't dance. At least not to the next song. He shows me pictures of his babies, who are hella cute. Doesn't take long before I feel bad for assuming he was looking for a quick trip to orgasm town. It's not that I've misjudged him so much as I didn't put any effort into getting to know him. Or anyone. If I sat down and had a conversation with Madison, it would probably turn out she's a good and multidimensional person too instead of the bossy queen bee I've pegged her as all weekend.

And Piper. I'm still mad at her, but maybe she hurt my pride more than anything. It was so much easier to believe I was too irresistible to stay away from instead of recognizing I was too emotional to be trusted. I did grow up under my mom's careful tutelage, after all. But Piper still slept with me without telling me the truth. We really need to sort that out if we're going to see each other again when we're back in the northeast. And I do want to see her again.

Except I don't even see her right now. Or at all through the rest of the night. I keep looking for her amid the dancing bridesmaids in their dusty pink dresses that are now hopelessly wrinkled. In the line at the bar and even in the women's bathroom. But she's not there. I ask Madison, and she looks at me like she doesn't even know Piper's name, and maybe I didn't misjudge her after all, but the bottom-line truth remains the same: Piper is gone.

As the party gets louder and my feet start to hurt, I walk back across the field where the resort staff have already taken down the chairs and decorations from the ceremony earlier. I expect Piper to be standing there in the clearing, like she's been waiting for me to finally get my head out of my ass. But she isn't. She's not at the top of the lift, where a sleepy attendant helps me get on a chair without dragging my dress on the damp ground. She's not at the bottom of the lift either, waiting to say she's sorry or that we should put our feelings aside and spend one more night together. The makeup sex would be pretty good, after all.

By the time I get back to the hotel, my confidence is failing. Was she angry? Hurt? Or maybe she's embarrassed about what we said to each other. If she were in front of me I'd say it doesn't matter, but she's not.

I make it all the way to her room at the end of a silent hallway and stand in front of the door with my hand raised to knock, but I can't make myself do it. If I could hear even the slightest noise inside—the sound of water running or the TV on or even feet pacing—I'd tap gently and see if she'd let me in, but there's no sign of her anywhere, and in the end, I go back to my shared room to wash off my makeup and call it a night. Enough damage done this week-end. If hooking up with Logan would have been a cliche, then banging on Piper's door, begging to be let in, is worse. Better to sleep it off and try again in the morning. We have brunch tomorrow before people leave. I'll be sure to save Piper a spot beside me.

13

When I wake up in the morning, my head aches from the joy of too much Sauvignon blanc and my heart hurts about the same.

Aunt Lois is sitting at the edge of her bed watching me like a hawk watches prey.

"Hi." The word is a croak, and I clear my throat. "What time is it?"

"How much therapy have you had in the last couple years?"

I groan. "So we're diving into it, then?"

She folds her arms over her chest. "That was a hell of a speech last night."

"Lois, I haven't even had any coffee yet."

We lapse into silence. I think about going back to sleep, but time's wasting, and I'd like to look mostly human when I come face-to-face with my family again. And Piper. Mostly Piper. I crack open one eye, and Lois is still watching me.

"Fine." I push myself up to sit against the headboard. "Let's have it."

She raises her palms. "Nothing to have. You said what you needed to say. But it sounded like there might be more where that came from. Maybe next time, share it with someone who is licensed to help you work through the feelings, rather than a room full of people who want to be told love is patient and kind."

I bury my face in my hands. "That was really embarrassing, wasn't it?"

"It was honest, kiddo, and weddings are the worst place for honesty. No one wants to be reminded that life is messy and marriage is hard at a wedding. It sounded like you came to some realizations last night, though. Would be a shame to let that go to waste. I went on a few dates with a psychologist from Westhampton last year. It didn't work, but I could give you her number if you want?"

This is far more conversation than I want to have so early in the morning. The only way to escape it will be in the shower, though I don't fully trust Lois not to follow me into the bathroom.

"I can find someone on my own, thanks."

She doesn't push it, and—mercifully—she doesn't follow. I turn the heat up as high as I can stand, trying to steam the hangover out. I need a clear head if I'm going to plead my case to Piper. And yeah, Lois is probably right. Therapy wouldn't be out of the question either. But that's something to deal with back in New York.

Brunch is at a diner in town. I drive with Lois and Grandma, Mom and Dad. The car is quiet. Grandma dozes next to me, and Mom has her head propped in her hand on the window ledge. I don't remember seeing her drink much, and I wouldn't put feigning a hangover for sympathy points past her, but Dad asks her if she wants to go back to the hotel twice before we park, so maybe it's legit.

There are more people than I expected as we walk in. Claire is standing in the door, shaking hands like a one-woman receiving line. It's weird that Jono isn't there with her, but the reason becomes apparent when she sees me approaching and breaks away from the well-wishers. She strides across the parking lot and links an arm through mine.

"I need to talk to you," she says.

Oh, shit. She doesn't look mad, exactly. But the way she walks us away from the restaurant and across the street to the same coffee shop Piper and I had breakfast in—God, was that only yesterday?—says we're not going to be negotiating either.

Still, she points at a table, and I sit down. She joins me a few minutes later with two coffees and two blueberry scones, setting one in front of each of us. I sit and watch her in silence, letting her set the tone. She picks agitatedly at her scone, breaking half of it down into crumbs, before finally she leans back in her chair and says, "Okay, let's have it."

"Have what?" I ask. We sound suspiciously like me and Lois not long ago.

"Whatever it is you think you need to say so we can go back to being sisters."

I blink. It's the most direct she's been with me since I came back from my trip.

"We're still sisters," I say, making a big production of pouring sugar into my coffee.

"Then can you please stop looking at me like bug guts on the windshield of your life, Kate? I didn't do anything wrong." She tears up, and I glance around, evaluating the people who are sitting enjoying their peaceful morning. Do they know the precipice Claire and I are standing on?

"We can't have this conversation here." I've hardly touched my coffee or scone, but I ball up the paper napkin and drop it on my plate.

"No, please." Claire puts a hand over mine. "Kate, come on, you have to forgive us sometime."

I settle again. I don't have to do anything, least of all when she starts issuing orders like that. But that stubbornness is part of how I got into this mess in the first place. Why Claire thought she needed to get Piper to be my minder for the weekend.

"I'm sorry," I say. "Please tell Jono I'm sorry."

She nods, and I hate it was that easy. But then she says, "We're sorry too. I'm sorry."

"I thought you didn't do anything wrong." It's harsher than I mean it to be. Old habits and all that.

She's pulled the second half of the scone apart, and now she's mashing it back into something like dough with her fork.

"I never slept with him while you were still together."

"I never said you did." Really though, I don't want to have this conversation in a public place.

"I didn't *do* anything wrong," she says again. "But there were lots of things I didn't not do either."

"You lost me." Double negatives are not my strong suit.

"I should have told you about me and Jono sooner. It was too easy not to. You were away, and it was so exciting being with him. You know what it's like, don't you? When you meet someone special. Especially someone you've known for a long time. It makes sense. It feels right."

I swallow, thinking of Piper. That was right. I know it. But instead of finding her and telling her that the things I overheard yesterday don't matter, I'm stuck sitting here letting Claire unburden herself.

"And then when you came back, it was too late. We were engaged. You were hurting. Everyone could see it. But I didn't know what to say. And then we moved, and it was like you running away, but in reverse."

"I didn't run away," I say.

"I'm sorry." She says it so fast I almost miss it. "I should have asked just once if you were okay."

This is the part where I tell her that's a weak-ass apology. That yes, she should have asked me even once if I had any strong feelings about her marrying Jono after he dumped me. That I hope she's happy now that she's married and got the wedding weekend of her dreams. I could even go so far as to say I hope she's happy out here in Colorado and that we'll see each other at Christmas and be nice for Mom and Dad's sake.

But those statements are really about me and my hurt feelings, and just like it's too late for Claire to ask if I'm okay, it's too late to dump on her the things I felt a year ago or longer. So I stick with objective facts instead.

"It was shitty to put Piper in the middle of this."

Here, at least, she gives me a grim smile. "I know. She told me so this morning before she left."

"She what?" My moment of triumph is cut short, and I nearly knock over my still-full coffee cup.

Claire shrugs, like nothing out of the ordinary has been said. Whatever Piper told her, she must have skipped over anything that wasn't totally PG-rated.

"She said she needed to get back. Something about a rush order for her jewelry."

My throat is tight. She was upset, sure. I knew that. But I didn't think she'd go so far as to run away.

I sigh. "We really made a mess, Claire."

"I know." She glances over her shoulder, toward the front door and across the street to the diner. "People are probably wondering where we are."

That's it. The moment is over. This is as close to an apology as I'm ever going to get, and I'll have to be happy with it. Time for that therapy Lois is such a strong supporter of.

So Claire surprises me when, instead of standing up and walking back to the party being thrown for her, she asks, "Do you want to come to Denver for a few days?"

"What?"

Her grim smile turns soft. "Come stay with us. Jonathan has to go back to work at the hospital tomorrow. We don't get a honeymoon until next year. Come spend a few days with me. We can talk some more. Get to know each other."

At face value, the idea of getting to know my sister seems silly. But give it a second glance, and it's not a terrible suggestion. I don't know her. Not this version of her. Not who she became after college and who she wants to be now that she's married and living so far from what was familiar growing up.

But every second I think about it is a second Piper gets farther and farther away. If I leave now, there might be some cinematic sprint through the airport so I can catch her and say I'm sorry. That it wasn't her fault, and that I shouldn't have said what I said.

Yet my story with Claire these last few years is about missed opportunities. If I say no today, she might invite me back again. Or she might not. There are only so many invitations and olive branches to extend, and Piper would probably be disappointed if I say no now. I have to tell myself that she'll understand. That if I reach out in a few days or a week and tell her that I stayed here to mend fences with Claire, Piper will know I did it in part for her, so that she never has to choose between me and her friend again.

"Sure," I say.

"Sure?" Her eyebrows go up so high it's funny, and they're lopsided because of her stitches, but I hurt a little at her surprise. How big a wedge have I driven between us that she didn't think I'd say yes?

"Yes, Claire. I'll come to Denver. We can have a sleepover and make brownies and watch movies."

Her smile is radiant. "Okay. Yes. Yes, that's good. Jonathan will be so happy too. He asked me like seven times last night after the reception if I was going to talk to you today."

"That's not what you were supposed to be doing on your wedding night," I say wryly.

"What? Oh." Her cheeks go pink, and she presses her fingertips to them. "Not like that. I mean . . . Kate. You're not supposed to say things like that."

I shrug. "Shouldn't have married Jono, then. I can give you some tips if you want. Do you know about the thing he likes where you take your finger and you—"

She's up like a shot. "Okay, time to go back to brunch."

No doubt the people around us are wondering what we were doing here if there's brunch elsewhere. Let them wonder. I follow my little sister who is now all grown up out of the coffee shop, taking steps that will hopefully lead to peace.

And hopefully someday soon I can find the way back to Piper.

14

SEVEN MONTHS LATER

IT'S TOO cold for a hike, but still, I pull into the lot at Storm King Mountain and take a minute to breathe. Pre-Christmas traffic is slow on the Taconic, and I should keep moving if I want to get to Mom and Dad's on time, but the detour feels necessary. I haven't been here since that day in med school, and coming alone now is part of my learning how to be with myself in familiar places.

Turns out Aunt Lois wasn't wrong about me needing therapy, and the woman in Westhampton is a hilarious mix of compassionate listening and a razor-thin tolerance for nonsense and bullshit. She does virtual appointments, and we talk every couple of weeks. Our conversations sometimes leave me feeling hollowed out and raw, and other times like I can accomplish anything. Being the overachieving eldest child is its own special kind of first-world trauma, and getting out from under it is a work in progress.

The road is quiet, and the late-December air pricks at my cheeks. I watch the puffs of air that escape my lips as I listen to bird calls and the passing swoosh of cars on the road. No one else stops, no doubt anxious to get where they're going.

The phone in my pocket rings. It's Mom. You can never truly be alone when Mom has a cellphone signal.

"Hello?"

"Kate? Where are you?"

Great Mom, thanks. How are you?

"I'm on my way. Probably another hour."

She sighs heavily. "We have to leave for Grandma's at three."

It's already two. Even on a clear day with no holiday traffic, I'll never get there in time. "Well, you'll have to go without me."

"Kate! Your grandmother will be so hurt if you don't show up."

"I'll see her tomorrow for Christmas dinner." In fact, she'll be at the house the whole day. Even when we were small, the rule was that gifts couldn't be opened until Grandma showed up. One year, Claire got impatient and started tearing paper off boxes in a tantrum. Mom was so committed to the not-until-Grandma-gets-here rule that she rewrapped them, and we had to pretend to be surprised when Grandma finally arrived and we opened the gifts all over again.

"But that's at our house," Mom says in exasperation. "She wanted to show you the new retirement residence."

I doubt that. The great drama of my family's last few months was the decision that it was time for Grandma to move to a residence. She's fought them every step of the way, but after a small kitchen fire right after Labor Day, she finally caved. Mom's been there every day, and Dad says most of their visits are Grandma complaining about the staff or the size of her room or the quality of the food, and Mom promising they'll find her somewhere new soon, even though she's literally staying in the best facility in town.

Another one of those little therapy nuggets I've learned is to be sympathetic to my mom, who has to cope with her own mother's demands, while still setting my own—very necessary—boundaries.

"I'll go see her on Boxing Day," I say. This visit with her today was dumped on me this morning as I was finishing my packing, and then when I said I wasn't sure I'd make it, Mom reacted like the sky was falling. The residence is holding a social event for families with eggnog and fruitcake, not a coronation. Whether I go or not will not spoil Christmas.

Mom hangs up still in a huff, but not before saying there's some leftovers in the fridge if I'm hungry when I arrive, which is a kind of coded forgiveness. If she were really upset, she wouldn't offer to feed me. She needs someone to acknowledge that she's working hard to keep the family sailing in one direction, even if sometimes we slip our lines and chart our own course.

There's an accident ten miles south of Storm King, which delays me even further. By the time I pull into the driveway, Mom and Dad's car is gone. Fine by me. I may be getting better at those precious boundaries, but having a few minutes to myself in their house will help me refortify before they get back.

It's weirdly silent, though I should get used to it. It's going to be a quiet Christmas. Claire and Jono are still in Denver and can't get home for the holidays. That was a whole other phone call with Mom, and a couple with Claire too. She was all set to fly here to spend thirty-six hours with us in order to appease Mom's disappointment, but after she and I talked a few times, I managed to convince her she wasn't responsible for that. It's her first Christmas with Jono, and she should be able to spend it with her husband if she wants to.

True to Mom's word, there are leftovers in the fridge. What we're missing is coffee. How she thinks anyone is going to get through the next few days without caffeine is unclear, but also something I can fix easily enough.

The supermarket is chaos with last-minute shoppers. For a second, I question how badly I really want to do this, but there's no way I can endure otherwise. Grandma's new health bugaboo is her cholesterol, which is no worse than her blood sugar, but she's insistent that something is wrong and that her time left with us is limited.

I've just grabbed a pack of beans when a voice behind my shoulder says, "Kate?"

For a second, I stay frozen, staring at the wall of coffee. If I don't turn around, she won't be there, and I won't have to examine the emotions the sight of her is going to dredge up inside me.

But the opposite side of setting up boundaries is pushing through the sticky parts inside of me that insist on clinging to difficult feelings.

The last time I saw Piper, she didn't look like herself. Between the anger on her face and the dress she'd have never worn otherwise, she was a stranger, even though her words cut in the way that only a scolding from someone you know and trust could. Today, she's very much herself. The one I thought I might get to know. The cat-eye glasses are back, and her hair is done up in a high ponytail and a checkered scarf. Her leather jacket looks butter-soft.

"Hi." I can't quite make myself look at her face for more than a second.

"Home for Christmas?" she asks.

"Yeah. You?"

"A few days, yeah."

And that's it. This is the small talk you make with people when you run into them at the grocery store. We'll go our separate ways and maybe repeat this holiday shopping exercise in five or ten years.

I don't want her to go.

"Claire's in Denver," I say quickly.

She nods. "I know. We talked yesterday."

Of course they did. She's always been Claire's friend. I try not to let the flash of resentment show on my face, but I must not be successful, because Piper's answer is a grimace that has us both dropping our gazes to the floor as shoppers flow around us.

"She says you two talk a lot too," Piper says, and the comment, as simple as it is, has my heart racing, because she's still here. It would be so easy to tell me to have a nice life, and yet we're still talking.

A woman with a shopping cart loaded down in Christmas dinner fixings clears her throat and glances meaningfully at the shelves of coffee. I dance away, accidentally brushing against Piper's jacket. She smells like leather and peppermint, and something like a flinch or a shiver ripples through her, but she brushes her hand over my hip in a way that's not entirely about keeping me steady. When our eyes meet again, the expression there isn't only friendly kindness either. It's the look she gave me at the bar while we flirted with straight guys. The one she used when we were trapped shoe shopping with Grandma.

Despite the time that's passed and the things we said, she still wants me.

"I'm sorry I never called," I say. Her lips thin as she wraps a hand around my wrist and tugs me down the aisle. She's carrying a shopping basket that has a bag of sugar and a bunch of rosemary in it. No doubt she's been sent on an emergency shopping expedition when someone realized key holiday ingredients were missing. She doesn't need my distraction. But she doesn't let go as we walk past the breakfast cereal and the peanut butter either.

Not calling after I got back from Colorado started out as an intentional thing. First because I didn't think she'd want to hear from me, then because it became clear I had my own shit to work through. No way was I going to put Piper in the middle of anything like my personal bridesmaid disaster again.

Then it became less intentional, because what was I supposed to say? *You were right and I'm sorry, and maybe you want to hookup again sometime?* Or else *I'm a mess, but maybe you're into mess?* So I stalked her Instagram and lusted after her new jewelry pieces and—okay—her, but I overthought it and wound up saying nothing.

So here we are, Christmas in Westchester, and once again I'm following after Piper like a kid on a leash, and I don't know how to make it more than that without admitting my bad behavior. And let's be honest, with Piper, it's all been bad behavior.

Ugh, baring my soul in the dairy aisle wasn't on my holiday wish list.

"About the wedding," Piper says.

"I'm sorry."

"I'm sorry."

"It's not that—"

"I would never—"

We babble sentence stems for a few seconds, dodging around the people trying to reach for eggnog and cottage cheese. Finally, as an old man who looks like he's dressed to climb Everest, not shop for frozen spinach, crashes his cart into Piper's ankles without so much as an apology, we break apart.

"I should get home," I say, holding up the bag of coffee

like it's a bomb that needs to be removed from the store before people get hurt. "How long are you in town for?"

"The day after Boxing Day," she says.

So fast.

"No rest for the wicked," I say. "Your new collection is awesome."

"You looked?" She flushes, her cheeks going a shade of pink I haven't seen since she shouted my name in that hotel room bed at the wedding.

"Of course," I say like it's the obvious answer, and it is. Regardless of what happened at the wedding, I've known her too long to not be curious about what she's up to. "I really like the feather earrings with the gold tips. They'd look great with your eyes." The last part slips out when I meant to keep it relatively impersonal, and I bite my lip to stop the apology that wants to follow. Better to say nothing.

Her smile is a happy, personal thing. It's not for me, but she's pleased, which warms me in turn. She asks, "What are you doing later?"

"Listening to Mom panic that the turkey won't be thawed in time, most likely," I say with an eye roll, then stamp down on that feeling too, because I'm trying really hard not to voice those thoughts aloud. They don't help, anyway. I shrug. "But nothing much. It's just us and Grandma, since Claire and Jono stayed out west."

She's eyeing me as I work through the explanation, but when I'm done, she says, "Come have a drink with me. I'll be at Dorothy's after nine."

Then she gets swallowed up by the current of shoppers sweeping through the store, and by the time I get myself turned down the same aisle, she's gone.

"Sounds good," I say to no one. "It's a date."

15

Leaving the house again that evening involves putting up with Mom's insistence that my departure will single-handedly ruin Christmas. I point out that she and Dad will be asleep in half an hour anyway and won't even notice I'm gone. This does not appease her.

"Kate's a big girl," Dad says calmly from where he's working on a crossword puzzle in his recliner. "Let her go have some fun."

Mom sulks the whole time I'm upstairs trying to figure out which of the only two outfits I've packed for this visit sets the right tone for "I'm sorry my emotional baggage fills a whole luggage rack, but also I still think about you more than childhood friends should."

Neither, as it turns out. Black jeans and black sweater. That's the best I've got.

Dorothy's is equal parts gay bar and coffee shop. Honestly, I've only been in a few times, always feeling like I was trespassing. Something else I'm working on with the therapist. I'm getting closer to owning this part of my identity and shedding who I thought I should be.

Piper is sitting in a round booth near the back. The place

is busier than I expected for Christmas Eve. She gives me a warm smile as she spots me crossing toward her, and it's only when I get to the table that I notice the small box with the red ribbon on it.

"Oh." My throat goes dry. "I didn't know we were doing gifts."

"It's nothing big," she says, but she pushes it aside, so maybe we're not doing gifts after all?

"You look great," I say. Unlike me, she must have packed for a month, because her jeans and jacket from earlier are gone, replaced by a mint green dress with sleeves that reach just below her elbows and a bateau neck that has a pretty bow off to one side, accentuating her collarbone. Her red lipstick has been switched out for a softer coral pink, but the effect still consumes all my attention for a moment, especially when she licks her bottom lip for a half second before she seems to catch herself.

We sit, and awkward silence squeezes in like an unwelcome party guest between us. For the first time, we're alone, with no chance of any family member barging in and demanding my attention, and all I can do is silently beg someone would come by and say "Piper? Is that you?" so I can buy time and figure out what exactly I've come here to say.

Since a distraction is inconveniently absent, the words I manage to piece together are, "Have you been seeing anyone?"

The corner of her mouth quirks up, but I can't tell if she's thinking of someone special or if my question is so obviously an attempt to get her to bring up what happened in Colorado that it's amusing.

"A few dates, off and on. Nothing serious. You?" Her arched eyebrow says, yeah, she knows what I'm doing, and she's lobbing the ball back into my court.

I shake my head, feeling shy. I've thought about it. Changed my settings on dating apps so that I can match with anyone, not only men. But any time someone messages me, regardless of gender, I don't reply. They're not Piper.

She slides the box with the ribbon over the table. "This is for you."

At first, I don't want to touch it. Because I don't have anything for her, and because somehow accepting a gift from her feels like goodbye. Like I'll get to keep whatever is in the box and not her. But it's not like I can really say no, so I pull the bow free and lift the lid to find a pair of earrings inside. Not just any earrings. The ones I mentioned. Feathers with tips dipped in gold. They're so delicate-looking that I can barely bring myself to touch them.

"You had these?" I ask. "How did you know?"

Her smile turns pleased. "I didn't. Let's just say there's one less box under the tree for my mom. But I had a few things for her, anyway."

I push the box away. "Oh, I can't do that. I don't want to take a gift away from your mom."

But she pushes it back to me. "Take it. They'll look amazing on you. With your skin tone, they'll—" She bites her lip, and the heat in her eyes is unmistakable. I want to fan those flames, but the odds I'll finally make an irreparable mess of things are so high that I can't move.

But Piper puts her hand over mine. Her palm is warm, and I flip my hand over so we can tangle our fingers together. The tickle of her fingertips makes me shiver, and my nipples harden under my sweater. Her lips part slightly, and with her free hand, she takes one of the earrings out of the box and drags the tip over the underside of my forearm.

"Piper," I say, and my voice is already thick.

"When Claire and I chat," she says without meeting my eyes, "she always mentions you. She tells me what you're up to and how often the two of you talk. Does she know about what happened at the wedding? With us?"

I shake my head. It's hard to speak because she's still trailing the golden feather on my skin. My fingers jerk and twitch, but she's still got my hand pinned down on the table under hers, so there's nothing I can do but try to control my breathing. The curve of the booth means most people can't see what we're doing.

"She's forgiven you," Piper says slowly. "And I only ever wanted things to be okay with the two of you. So I'm sorry for what I said at the wedding. And what I did."

"What you did?" I ask. My skin is on fire.

"I should have been honest about what Claire asked me to do. That wasn't fair to you. And it made things complicated."

The feather stills. When her gaze finally lifts to mine, there's need there. Want. But also worry, like I might not forgive her for whatever she thinks she's done.

"No more complicated than I made it. Than I've always made it." As I speak, she starts moving the earring again, and my toes curl inside my boots. "But Piper, if you don't stop doing that, I'm going to crawl under this table and up your skirt, and people can watch if they want to."

The catlike satisfaction that spreads over her face matches the pointed corners of her glasses perfectly.

"Why do you think I'm doing it?"

She's back. The Piper from the wedding. The powerful woman who grew out of the endearing teen I used to know. Faced with her, there's nothing I can do but melt. I ball my free hand into a fist as my breathing goes shallow.

"Should we go somewhere else?" I ask.

"I really think we should."

———

Easier said than done. We start by getting into my car. There are some attempts at making out, but the front seat of a Ford hatchback is not exactly spacious. Then, some conversation about where we should go, since sneaking around either of our parents' houses is less than ideal. But what with it being Christmas Eve, the closest hotel or Airbnb that isn't charging a small fortune is halfway back to Albany, and the restless way Piper keeps picking at and smoothing down her skirt tells me she isn't willing to wait that long either.

So in the end, I wheel the car around and head back to Mom and Dad's. Only the porch light is on as we blunder our way up the walk. I trip on the top step and Piper has to hold me upright, then we laugh as I fumble with the keys, and finally, I drag her inside.

"Come here," I whisper, pulling her face to mine as the door slams shut. I shush it, then laugh more at the idea of shushing an inanimate object. Piper shakes against my kiss, trying to quiet her laughter too. Her fingers are icy as she slides her hands under my sweater, and I arch, trying to get away, but it only presses me more against the rest of her, and the throaty huff she makes says that was her plan all along.

A creaking sound upstairs is the only thing that pulls me away from her long enough to take a breath. We both freeze, eyes cast upward. If someone comes down for a midnight snack, it's going to be hard to explain what we're doing. But the house is silent aside from the whir of the furnace.

"This way," I say softly, tugging her away from the door. She goes toward the stairs, and it takes a second before I realize she's going toward my old bedroom. The one that is a craft nook now. So I pull a little harder and lead her through the living room to the stairs that go to the basement. We've done this once before, back when I was spinning out of control and Piper was the only one who noticed. Tonight, I hope to be more in charge. Of myself and of what's still between us.

"So much better," she says as we make our way down. The basement has been finished since Claire and I were kids. Most of it is a workshop for my dad and a laundry room, but there is also a bedroom at the bottom of the stairs that functions as a guest room. We're barely inside before Piper is lifting the sweater over my head and I'm bunching her skirt in my fists, trying to reach the soft skin beneath.

It's like riding a bike or falling off a horse. We fall into each other, tumbling down to the mattress and squirming out of our clothes with no finesse. As polished as Piper is in all other circumstances, now she's only hot and eager. I move my hands restlessly over her body, and she makes soft desperate noises as I nip at her skin.

"Kate. Please." She is lying on her back with her hair spread around her on the pillow. Her breasts are creamy peaks that I could play with all night, but she's already got one hand between her thighs, and it seems entirely unfair that she gets to have that privilege. When I caress over her stomach, she pulls her hand away, leaving me to explore the slick heat between her folds. She's so wet, and I groan at the thought that she feels this much for me. Despite everything, she still wants me.

"More," she says, grabbing hold of my wrist, trying to guide me where she needs me, but I know it won't be enough. Instead, I slide further down as Piper pushes up so she's leaning against the headboard, legs spread wide and ready for me.

Tasting her is as perfect as it was last time, and she lets out a relieved moan when I tongue her clit for the first time. Her whole body rolls at the contact, and I spread her labia wider so I can have full access. I take my time, listening to the way she sighs and how her breath punches out of her as

I circle around her. When I slip a finger inside, she rocks restlessly, and I do my best to find what she needs. I try to feel confident. I've touched myself enough with her in mind to know what should feel good. And some part of it must be working, because she's panting encouragement as I lave and lick.

"Kate. Kate." Each time she says my name, it's a breathy staccato sound. "More. Your tongue. More."

I follow her instructions, and she tenses underneath me. Her heels are on my back and she pushes down, trying to drive her hips up against my mouth, until finally, her whole body flexes as she gasps and spasms around my fingers. She grips my hair, holding me close until she's taken the pleasure she needs, and as her hold relaxes, I slide free, nipping at the sensitive skin on the inside of each thigh and enjoying the way she squeaks and jerks.

She purrs and kisses me when we're face to face again, then slides a thigh between my legs. Her fingers find my nipples, and they tease and pinch with expert skill. I hope we get to do this often enough that I know exactly what to do to turn her on as fast as she does me. As I really start to whine, she puts a hand over my mouth. We're two floors down, so there's not much chance of us being heard, but the idea that we have to be quiet gets me even more excited than I already am.

I throw my head back, tossing it around until I can get my mouth free. "More," I say, echoing her own command from a minute before.

She laughs, nuzzling against my armpit, before she mutters, "Okay, okay."

There's no preamble as she slides two fingers inside me, but the shock of it has me gasping as I widen my legs, trying to leave all the room I can for whatever it is she wants to do. I expect her mouth, but she holds off, working her fingers in and out, twisting and thrusting. Once, she brushes over a spot that sends sparks over my nerves, and when I gasp, she gives me her creamy cat smile.

"Found it," she says, then brushes over it again. Unlike my attempts, her movements are certain, working me up to a place I've never felt before.

"Piper. You're amazing." That's what I try to say, but it comes out more like a series of garbled grunts and sounds as heat builds at my center. I need to come. My whole body is moving, straining for it. My hips are rocking against her fingers, so she hardly needs to do anything as she strokes that fiery place inside me.

"Okay?" she asks.

I could come like this. But her question has me circling my clit, trying to find the top of this peak. Piper makes a *tsk*ing noise before she smacks my hand away and takes over, running her thumb in tight circles over me.

"Yes." Oh God, yes. What's about to happen is something I've never felt before. My body coils, overcome with a sensation like a hot wash that starts at the back of my head and pours over my scalp and down my entire body. Piper works me through it as I cry out and shake and shudder. The orgasm leaves me feeling electrified, and she keeps going, taking me to another climax I don't even feel coming. I stuff a fist as far into my mouth as I can manage, because even two floors of wood and insulation won't completely muffle my scream. And finally, I have to beg her to stop because I'm so sensitive that I can't seem to stop the aftershocks that rock through me over and over.

Piper wraps me up in her arms as I gasp against her warm skin. I may have started crying at some point, because she swipes her thumbs over my cheeks. My throat is sore, and she kisses my neck. She knows each place to touch. Every spot that needs care.

"You're so perfect, Kate," she says, and in that moment, I might even believe it. I feel shiny. Polished. "I've wanted you my whole life, and now, I have you."

If it's like that every time, she very well might.

———

I DON'T THINK either of us plan for Piper to stay over, but whenever the mood shifts and one of us rolls toward the edge of the bed like we might start making our goodbyes, the other reaches and pleads and kisses until the air changes again and there are no more thoughts of leaving. We don't talk much, not about big things, the past or the future. We share little stories. Me, about my travels. Piper, about the new collection she's working on, with shapes and colors inspired by our weekend in Colorado.

"After Claire has the baby, maybe we can go back out there and spend some real time," I say, kissing her shoulder.

"Baby? What baby?"

I press my smile into her skin. I was sworn to secrecy on that little jewel. It's part of the reason she didn't want to travel for the holidays, but it's still very early for her and Jono. She made me promise not to tell another soul, but what she really meant was not to tell Mom. I know Piper can keep a secret.

After the appropriate amount of squeeing and exasperation that Claire hasn't told Piper about the pregnancy, we settle back into each other's arms and fall asleep. It's very late—or early, depending on how you look at it—and I'm so exhausted and blissed out that I'm barely swimming back up to consciousness as footsteps on the stairs come toward me. There's a warning *tap tap* on the door, and I'm still pushing up to my elbows and realizing I have not a single stitch of clothing on and that Piper is just as naked sprawled out next to me, with her swan tattoo exposed for all to see, when my mom barges into the room.

"Kate, honey, are you getting up any time today? It's Christmas morning, and I have to go get Grandma and—"

The description of someone's eyes going so wide they nearly fall out of their head is only a metaphor, but honestly, Mom tries her best to do it. She rocks so hard on her feet I think she's been punched by an invisible fist, and she has to steady herself against the wall. Her face goes pale, and my shoulders bunch as I prepare to defend myself— and Piper's honor too.

"Morning, Lee," Piper says. Her voice is sleepy, and her cheek is wrinkled with the imprint of a pillow. And she's called my mom "Lee" a hundred thousand times over our lives, but today it's filled with a mature self-assuredness that says we're all adults here and there's no need to make a big deal about this. I wonder again and again how Piper became this person when I'm still scrambling to form any sort of words with my brain, much less my mouth. More questions for therapy, I guess.

"Kate." Mom's eyes narrow. She would never scold a guest, not even one she's known since childhood, but I'm fair game. "It's Christmas."

And I stare at her, bracing for the lecture about how my proclivities have ruined the holidays and what will we tell Grandma? But she only continues gaping and blinking like her indignation has gone offline, leaving nothing but a blank. Piper squirms down under the cover and drapes an arm over my stomach, and the silent support keeps me from lashing out like I might have in the past. We don't need to defend or explain what's happening here. It hasn't ruined anything, and Grandma will have to live with it. She's always liked Piper, anyway.

Finally, Mom clears her throat and runs her hands over

the fuzzy snowman sweater she wears every year on Christmas morning. She says, "Your father made coffee. Piper, stay as long as you want, unless your family needs you."

"Thanks, Lee," Piper says, and she must be using Mom's name intentionally to remind her of their long-standing relationship and that none of this needs to be weird.

Mom's gaze catches mine, and despite Piper's wordless reassurance and my months of hard work with the psychologist, I still flinch internally at her silent judgment. I can already hear the lecture later about causing a spectacle, even though there is literally no one down here to see us but her, and even that could have been avoided if she'd bothered to give me the privacy I'm due as an adult. But all she says is, "Merry Christmas, honey."

Her footsteps back upstairs go a little faster than when she came down. Piper and I both stare up at the ceiling, waiting for the muffled but no doubt agitated monologue that will come when she tells my dad what she's seen. And it does come, a high-pitched and rapid-fire string of words, followed by Dad's slower and calmer ones. We can't actually hear what they're saying, but Dad's almost certainly reminding her that firstly, I'm a grown-up who makes my own decisions and have been for quite some time. Next, he'll say that Piper is a good girl who they've known for more than twenty years. Finally, he'll round it out with the reminder that wouldn't Mom rather I date someone they know and trust than to have me call from a country several time zones away to say I'm in love with a stranger they've never even heard of and won't be coming back? At which point Mom will pout and go back to stuffing the turkey because, after all, the most important thing to remember today is that it's Christmas, and we can't possibly sit down for dinner any later than four p.m. or else Grandma will have a heart attack midway into diabetic shock.

"Merry Christmas," Piper says, kissing my cheek and drawing me out of my thoughts. I laugh as I turn to kiss her properly.

"You're sticking around for a bit, right?" Despite all my intentions of staying strong, I could use her support. Today. Maybe for longer. A lot longer.

"Are you kidding?" She rests her chin on my shoulder, looking up at me with warm bedroom eyes. "Lee said I can stay as long as I want. You don't get an offer like that every day."

You definitely don't. Piper's been in my life for as long as I can remember, but this version of us, wrapped up in each other, makes me feel like we've finally reached our destination.

I hope we get to stay here for years to come.

THE END

ABOUT THE AUTHOR

Allison lives in Toronto with her very patient husband and the world's cutest team of rescue pets. She tries to split her time between writing, exploring Toronto's parks, and traveling anywhere that has good wine. Tragically, this leaves no time to clean the house.

CONTEMPORARY ROMANCES BY ALLISON TEMPLE

Out & About

Work-Love Balance

Honeymoon Sweet

The Seacroft Series

Top Shelf

Cold Pressed

Hot Potato

Shared Series

Puppuccino (part of Bold Brew)

Standalone

Destination Bedding

The Neighbourly Thing

Up North

Boyfriend With Benefits

The Pick Up

LGBTQ+ FANTASY BY ALLI TEMPLE

The Pirate & Her Princess

Uncharted

Unbroken

Unleashed